PREY 4 KEEPS

Copyrights 2025 Vernon Grimes lll

VNature Rarebreed

All rights are reserved. Printed in the United States of America. No part of this book shall be used or reproduced in any manner whatsoever without written permission except in the case of brief quotations embodied in critical articles or reviews.

This book is a work of fiction. Names, characters, businesses, organizations, places, events, and incidents either are the product of the author's imagination or are used fictitiously. And resemblance to the actual persons, living or dead, events or locals is entirely coincidental.

For information contact: Phabonyx@gmail.com

Vernon Grimes lll/VNature Rarebreed/Lil V Nature

Editing by Vernon Grimes/VNature Rarebreed

Instagram/Vnature919

Facebook/VNature Rarebreed

Lil V's Acknowledgements

I gotta give thanks for being able to continue to wake up and be healthy enough to bring these stories to light. Thanks to all my family and relatives. Grimes family. My 9-year-old niece Trisha, who fussed me out bc her name wasn't in my book Bartholomew. My niece Tiera, nephew, Zah'Quez and Nazaiah, who are all too young to read this book. It's not suited for kids at all. My aunts and uncles. The Dukes, The Alstons, The Boose, The Winters, The Fox's, The Cooley's, Ticia Lucas. Bradley's, The Barbee Family, Fox's, Suzette, My sisters and brothers, Misha, Nicci, DJ Dezerk, Purple, Raeshawn, Tony, Trenton, Quinton. My parents. Grandma Irene. My daughter Teari. My son Ve'son. My biggest I'mere. Troy, Lamont Hocutt. My homie Lil Kev from Swain, Joi and the whole family. All my people in Worthdale. All my old childhood neighbors from Beverly to Burgundy to Rawls. Classmates from Powell, Bugg, Ligon, Mt. Vernon Redirection, Enloe, Mary Phillips. Any of my old cellmates, bunkies, anybody I crossed paths with doing county and Fed time. Shout out to the black owned businesses like CAPS Fashion Boutique in Southgate. Shout out Curt Raw. Any and everybody who always sends positive vibes my direction. To everybody at my job All American Relocation. Rest in peace to all the ones we lost early in Raleigh. Shout to the whole Bull City, Fayettenam, G-Vegas. The whole southeast to the north and west Raleigh for pushing the culture forward, music and movies. M1 from Dead Prez for sending me that verse on Dorothea Dix. All the barbershops on the southside. All the black owned food spots and bars. Fat Boys, Liquid Legends, Oak City Fish, Jacks Seafood, Touchdown. I know it's a lot more I could name. Stay focused and stay motivated. Long live KK Kenyejah Grimes-Pulley, Ryan, Mook Dig, Jamari (Trouble) Travis Taylor (Goo), Terrel House (Dyce), Lil Tierra, Akim (Fat Cat) and Crystal Pulley, Trey Flip. Extra shout out to Freeze from Detroit who told me to stop bullshittin on the yard in Herlong, California medium and told me to write some books so I would have something when I go home. I saw you on a movie you made too it was krazy bc I just so happened to walk in and see you on the big screen. Shout out to my very own O56. Can't forget the 057s and 058s. Big shout out to Two Hunnit yea!!! If y'all don't know he always pushed the culture and the music first for the city and branded it. The whole 9Deuce for always branding Raleigh. Everybody locked up, hold your head and write them books or them movie scripts. Don't be afraid to let people know that you can read and write. You still gone be a gangsta. Let's make what's right popular again. Big Thanks to everyone everywhere and even the smallest of contributions!!!

The year: Spring 2007

The place: Southeast Raleigh

"The lingo might switch. The players may pass away or change, but the results remain the same."

-Lil V

Contents

1. A.M. Drama — 1
2. Closed Mouths — 7
3. Family Itch — 13
4. Daddy's Throne — 18
5. Ice Grill — 22
6. Bait — 28
7. New Era — 36
8. Knows Best — 41
9. Body-talk — 45
10. Blue Nights — 52
11. Rough House — 59
12. Rotten — 66
13. Laundry Money — 73
14. Trails — 80
15. Hard Head — 86
16. Salty — 92
17. Missfits — 98
18. Farfetched — 104
19. Young Pain — 110
20. Headlights — 116

21. Sight's Set	122
22. Breathe Easy	127
23. Salute	134
24. Conflict	141
25. Roadblock	147
26. Blinded	152
27. Alarms	158
28. Burned	163
29. Eye's Wide	168
30. Last Dance	173
31. The Letter	177
About The Author	181

PREY 4 KEEPS

x

VNature Rarebreed

Chapter 1

A.M. Drama

"That shit both y'all got going on need to stop, Joanne!" Crystal demanded, waving her index finger around wildly.

"What shit, Crystal? It's way too early for your bullshit this morning!" Joanne stood with her arms crossed in her violet robe.

Crystal's eyes walked up and down Joanne's curvy figure. She hated it when the prettiest people carried the ugliest attitudes and Joanne was one of the types she despised.

"You and Antwan. That's what. Don't play stupid with me! My brother went and upgraded yo' ass when you ain't have a pot to piss and window to throw it out of. And this is how you thank him, huh?"

Crystal stood firm, making her point on the front porch of her brother's home. Luckily, he was out of town on business, and no one would have to explain all the early morning commotion for now.

Joanne's life was a miserable wreck before she met Tyrone Hunter; often referred to as Quiet Storm. She fled her undesirable past in Detroit, Michigan, which landed her in the Bull City, Durham, North Carolina. He had his first encounter with her three years ago, during a drop-off in one of Bull City's housing projects.

Joanne was sleeping on a few blankets on the floor which she had fluffed up to make her stay comfortable. A couple of baby diapers were on the edge of the makeshift mattress she made, but all Tyrone could notice was the face and body of a goddess before him.

***

"Man, what's up with ol' girl downstairs, Buttafly?" Tyrone interrogated the man who he'd just handed four and a half ounces of powder cocaine.

The man was a slim, brown skinned brother, with the same wavy texture of hair as the man on the Sportin' Waves can. Although he only had the voice to match, people in the city often called him Keith Sweat.

Keith Sweat was a local cane dealer, and what Tyrone assumed to be an undercover homosexual. Not one to concern himself with another man's sexual orientation, he guessed the intriguing figure on the floor was not of the downlow brother's taste. He wanted answers.

"Man, that's my sister, Ieisha's friend. She ain't got nowhere to stay right now so, I let 'er shack here." Buttafly removed the grape blow pop that he was sucking on from his mouth.

"She cleans up when she ain't sleeping, nonstop. I think she got that OCD. And did I mention, can cook too? She a bad ass bitch. Got no man neither." Buttafly stuck the blow pop back onto his tongue after twirling the stick on his fingertips.

Buttafly stood there as if he had just auctioned off a slave with his palm open. Tyrone slapped his open right palm.

When Tyrone came back downstairs, things were beginning to gleam as Joanne swiveled the mop across the floor. She was still in her sleeping attire, a cotton candy blue tank top and pink cotton candy boy shorts. Her private parts looked as if it had her crouch area of the fabric in a tight mooseknuckle lock.

"Have mercy!" Tyrone mumbled louder than intended.

Joanne quickly looked up, catching him in his gaze, then went back to cleaning. She was used to receiving all types of attention from men, even women at times.

"How you doing, beautiful?" Tyrone greeted and was met with a bewildered look.

"You talking to me? Because I'm looking a hot mess," the tainted but surely astonishing Joanne quizzed.

"Yea, of course. Who else would I be?" he stuck out his hand.

"Tyrone. I'm Butta's people," he said to imply that he was trustworthy.

"You like comedy, right? Come with me to Goodnight's, Katt is in town. Tickets on me," Tyrone went into his pocket retrieving the invitations.

Buttafly was just now descending to the bottom of the stairs, wrapping a colorful button up collared shirt onto his frame. He wanted to get more of an earful, but mainly to play matchmaker.

"Uh, I don't know. I got my daughter, Tanisha and everything," Joanne replied before she was cut off by Buttafly.

"Awl, girl, don't be silly. You know Ieisha 'll keep an eye on her for you, girl," he suggested with his right hand hanging loosely and his left hand on his hip.

Tyrone wondered how Buttafly could survive such a treacherous game with the obvious feminine ways he was displaying. Normally, not so persistent, he tried convincing Joanne for a second time.

"I take it that maybe you thank Katt must've fell off. It's cool, I'll see if my auntie is busy this weekend. She like Katt Williams. Get at me when you ready, Butta," he said, making way to the front door.

Buttafly winked and nodded in Tyrone's direction as he left, giving Joanne the green light.

"Look, don't give up that easy. I love a little comedy," Joanne said, cracking a strained smile. Tyrone didn't have the slightest idea just how overjoyed she really was to be asked out.

Tyrone pulled from his back pocket a business card and handed it to Joanne along with a ticket to the event.

"Alright, I see you. Quiet Storm's Tow and Recovery," she read aloud the card with his contact on the bottom.

"That's my personal line. Text me your number if you don't mind. I left my phone in the truck," Tyrone backed up towards the screen door.

"I'll see you later, uh. You know what, I never did get your...," he paused, rubbing his natural waves a bit embarrassed.

"Name? That's ridiculous. You messing up already. It's Joanne," she filled her name into Tyrone's blank.

"Alright, ok, Joanne. You got me. Believe me, I'm on point now. Yo' fine ass," Tyrone mumbled as he pushed the handle on the door, making his exit.

"That's an old ass name," he said to himself as he walked towards the black wrecker truck with gray letters.

Buttafly walked over to bring himself closer to Joanne. He palmed her soft, right cheek as if he were heterosexual.

"He sure as hell better be on point with any of my bitches," he said as he and Joanne shared a laugh.

***

"That's ridiculous!" Joanne laughed off the accusation.

"But you know what? I hear you Cryssy. You have made it loud and clear. I'll keep little don't-nobody-want-his-ass, Twan from over here!" Joanne spat irritated and ready to get the conversation over with.

"Even though, we ain't got shit going on. But to save what me and Ty got, that's what I'll do for you. So, you feel better now, this morning Crystal? Is there anything else I can do for you? I have grits on the stove."

"Yea, that'll work for me. But you know if Tyrone thought y'all did have something going on, somebody getting fucked up!" Crystal promised as she stepped down from the porch and began to scrape her bedroom slippers on the street.

For a Thursday morning, Joanne was already bombarded with enough drama to not need to hear anything else negative for the rest of the day.

"Crystal's boney, crackhead ass better mind her fuckin' business if she knows what's good for 'er. I need a shot early and it's barely even six thirty in the morning. She got me messed up," she said angrily as she lit up the cigarette wedged between her two fingers.

"What did Crystal want?" Dirty interrogated as he approached from behind.

"Boy, you know what she wanted. She wanna get back on that pipe. I told 'er you ain't have shit, though. But I know you need to slide back in that room before my daughter see your ass. You know she about to leave out for school in a minute," Joanne said, pushing her palm into his bare chest.

Dirty turned around and did as Joanne had asked, leaving her to herself. She took a long drag on the cigarette before blowing out the chain of smoke.

"Fuck Crystal! I'm a grown ass woman," she vented stepping inwards and shutting her home's door.

Chapter 2

Closed Mouths

The smell of the medical dispensary weed permeated the air throughout the hallway, edging its way towards Tanisha's room. She loved the aroma of the high-grade weed but was forbidden to indulge during school hours by her mother's rules.

At 13, she had covered more ground than some 20-year-olds, but that was another thing she kept safely guarded. Feeling some type of way about not being able to smoke and being treated like a child, she vented her frustrations.

"Fuck y'all mu'fuckas! Y'all ain't gotta let me smoke. Shit, I got my own," she said aloud over the Pretty Ricky album that was echoing off the walls in her room.

The young, but experienced teen had an innocent schoolgirl look about herself, especially, with her Shirley Temple curls. Her breast was small, but hips were beginning to widen ahead of everything else.

Tanisha dug into the small bra and pulled from it a clear bag full of budded up light green nuggets.

"Ah ha!" She celebrated aloud to herself as she raised the grape flavored blunt wrap, she'd scavenged her cluttered room for.

"What the hell Ta Ta in there yelling about?" Dirty jumped from the edge of the bed and passed Joanne the lit blunt.

Joanne suffocated the flame in a nearby ashtray.

"Wait, Twan. You think you slick. I see you trying to ease your way out of here 'fore I ask you where the rest of my shit again," she spat, grabbing hold of her nephew's elbow.

"What shit, Anne?" he quizzed as if he didn't know already.

"Dirty Twan don't play with me. I'm missing a blunt I rolled up and a quarter of that same shit we just smoked. I'm gone fuck your lil ass up you keep messing with my shit! Boy, if you won't my husband Ty's nephew...," she paused, raising her fist then resting it back onto the bed.

"Well, ain't got it. But since you swear I do got it, I'll take care of you later on. All these accusations making me hungry," Dirty told his uncle's fiancée.

Joanne responded with an unconvinced expression on her face as she went into a childlike disposition.

"No, Twan. You need to take care of me right now." Joanne slid closer to the edge where Dirty was standing.

"And how I'm 'posed to do that?" he questioned.

"You know nigga. You grown right? I'm hungry too," she said with a sinister look on her face.

Joanne was swift as a cat with her right hand as she grabbed Dirty's unerect package. She looked into his dark-black pupils. She began stroking her hand back and forth as he stood in his Jordan Brand athletic shorts. The sensation of her fingertips up against his manhood sent electric impulses throughout his muscular frame.

Dirty loved getting high with his uncle's fiancée. From head to toe, she was a stallion. She owned long, natural, jet-black hair that hung down to the middle of her back, which she wore slicked back into a tight ponytail. Her skin was an evenly brown tone; smooth and unblemished.

Her eyes were dark and chinky, due to her grandmother's Asian descent, but her lips were full of her African heritage. 37-27-42 were Joanne's measurements. She was undeniably irresistible to a holy man, who wasn't hugging his bible close to his chest.

With a name like Dirty, you couldn't ask Antwan Clee Hunter to be diplomatic. Any opportunity not taken was not guaranteed to present itself again. Hence, a distant uncle and a lonely Joanne was a perfect day for him.

Dirty began to grow larger and stronger underneath his shorts as Joanne continued her stroke. She admired his 5'10 athletic frame with her eyes, while her left hand traveled across his 6 pack gently.

His manhood was throbbing inside the palm of her hand like a hot heartbeat. He removed Joanne's hand to slide his shorts to his knees so that she could gain better access. She took his bulging flesh and rubbed it on the side of her face to feel the warmth.

"You want to see what I got underneath this robe, baby?" she asked as she began to play with the sticky wetness between her thighs.

Dirty said yes with a simple lick of his lips as she untied the knot, revealing what quickly sprung Tyrone. Her flawless and curvaceous body was the hook and sinker.

Joanne wore a red see through Teddy with black trim and straps that connected from her panties to red stockings. It was originally to be showcased for Tyrone when he came home from his business venture, but her hunger couldn't survive the times he constantly put her through.

Joanne dropped to her knees and grabbed Dirty by his backside with both hands and guided his stiffness into her wet mouth.

She sucked away at his rod causing pre-cum to ooze into the back of her throat. Her insides became as slippery as black ice with every thrust inside of her mouth.

"Mmmh!" she moaned as her heartbeat increased rapidly from the excitement.

"You taste good! You been eating peaches too," she mumbled as spit fell from the right side of her mouth.

Joanne rose from her knees and crawled on the bed like a feline. With Dirty studying, she stood on all fours as her cheeks parted on their own, like Crabtree Mall entrance doors. The youngster's eyes grew wide at the sight of the soft baby hairs and pink inner lips perched out.

Dirty wasn't experienced in the munching field so, he went straight for what he knew best in his eighteen years. He rubbed his thirsty main vein between her slot as it opened up for him.

"Go ahead, Twan, baby. Fuck this pussy!" Joanne begged.

He began to push inside of her slippery slopes, thumbs parting her soft, round cheeks. Joanne lowered her face into the plush, goose feather pillows and arched her back to feel an even deeper penetration.

"Unh, Twan," she moaned his name frequently.

"Hold on. Hold on," she stopped him, realizing that she needed to cover her tracks.

She jumped up to lock the unsecured room door. Then, she grabbed the remote to her cd player and pressed play on the R. Kelly TP-2.com album.

"Okay," Joanne said to put things back in motion.

"Baby, grab my neck," she uttered as Dirty slid his stiffness back inside of her.

Joanne made it very clear to him that she liked it rough. He obliged, gripping her throat as he slammed harder and deeper to touch her spot.

Her brown cheeks collided against his cut, pecan brown abdominals, causing cum to splatter onto his 6-pack as she orgasmed multiple times. The 31-year-old, more experienced Joanne called for the 18-year-old Dirty to release inside of her quickly. They were both walking a thin line, but she was pressed for time, and surely on point with her birth control.

"Hurry up, baby. We ain't got much time. Get you, baby!" Joanne warned.

She predicted that Tyrone would pop up earlier than he'd promised as he always did in the past. And if he didn't, she had to handle the office work at the garage for him.

Dirty dug into her with eight hard, long strokes. Loads of cream ejaculated into her gushy, warm slot. They both fell limply onto the bed for a brief moment, until Joanne shoved him off of her quickly.'

"I got to take a shower so I can get to work on time. And you, need to be gone about your business!" she urged as she threw on her robe.

"You know, if you want to keep on fuckin' this pussy, closed mouths get fed," she said, rushing towards her bathroom.

Dirty quickly put his clothes on then headed out of the bedroom door.

"Yea, lil cutty must of bounced out to school already," he said, stopping to push open Tanisha's room door.

The pink and white ensemble was neat and tidy. So many characters of stuffed animals were aligned, covering half of her bed, but no sign of the teenager. Dirty closed the door and strutted off, feeling invigorated.

Tanisha was no further than the home across from her residence. She watched Dirty as he walked along the limestone walkway in her mother's yard. Soon, he disappeared down the Raleigh street, past the teens loading onto their school buses.

Dirty and Joanne smoked weed together on numerous occasions. It never crossed Tanisha's mind that anything would transpire besides the two getting high with each other. Besides, she and her best friend were about to do the same as she watched the school bus take off without them.

Chapter 3

Family Itch

Crystal started feeling herself give in to her own temptations. Slowly, she had been refraining from her addiction for nearly three months. She had also been doing hair at Sheryll's, a local salon school. And she began getting great reviews for her work which led to more clientele.

But just as her achievements began to stack up, her demons found their way to the forefront again. Now, the money that she needed to pay for hair products and booth rent became more feasible for getting high.

A knock at the door disturbed the sleep of Crystal's nephew.

"Twan, it's me, Crystal," she whispered through the crack of the door.

Dirty wiped the slobber from the side of his mouth, then lifted himself from the bed. It had only been an hour and a half since he'd left Tyrone's house around the corner. And he hadn't planned on coming out of his shell until nightfall hit. He approached the door, rubbing his testicles, then cracking the door slightly.

"What's up, Cryssy? What the hell you want all early and shit?" he asked, still scratching his nuts.

Crystal gave her nephew a distasteful look.

"You got something, lil nigga?" she replied.

"Nawl! Ain't got shit! Fuck you mean?" Dirty reacted offensively.

"I was just scratching my nuts to be scratching 'em. Some man shit. You wouldn't know nothing about it," he said, trying to move the conversation along.

"Boy, ain't talking 'bout them crabs you got. I'm talking about some hard," she retorted.

"Nawl, ain't got none of that neither," he said, no longer toying with himself.

Crystal looked at her nephew in disbelief as she crossed her arms and smacked her lips.

"Now, come on, Antwan Clee. You know I know better, nephew. Ty don't leave out of Raleigh without leaving you with nothing," Dirty's aunt implied that she knew her brother and nephew's operation.

"I know you trynna keep me on the right path, but I don't need you for that. I can do that on my own. I been going to SouthLight. And besides, it ain't for me. It's for Jeff. He gave me some extra money to see if I could get it for him. Now, come on, now. Stop playing, Twan," she continued to plead.

"For real, I'm not playing Crystal. If I had it, you would know, because you would get it. Besides, Ty been gone all week long," Dirty responded.

The urge that Crystal had didn't want her to believe him no matter what his excuse was. He was holding out. It appeared that he wanted to see his aunt kick the habit, but that wasn't the case. He really was out of drugs to sell and only halfway cared about her relapsing.

Dirty knew that Crystal would come fiendin' sooner or later. He figured if not him, she'd get it from somewhere. He loved his aunt loosely and had a funny way of showing it. Low-key, he felt she was the reason his father got addicted to drugs, making his childhood difficult.

Crystal shared the same bloodline as Tyrone "Quiet Storm" Hunter. She was born into this world as the one-minute older twin sister to Dirty's now deceased father, Clearance Cleon "Clee" Hunter. Clee suffered from cancer, spending his last years on chemotherapy and continuing to abuse drugs and alcohol. He and his twin shared many things growing up from their looks to their drug habits. And now, Crystal was chasing her twin to the grave.

"I'm about to go back to sleep. Your nephew done had a rough night," Dirty put his fist to his mouth and yawned.

"Nigga, please. I doubt it," she spat in a cynical tone of voice.

"Eating pussy and getting your lil ass meat sucked is not what I call a rough night or morning. You act as if I don't know about what you really been up to."

Dirty gave his sister a skeptical look in hopes she would elaborate more on that last remark.

"I thank you and Joanne been messing around in the dark. Don't play with me, Antwan! I'm literally holding yo' life in the palm of my hands," Crystal said, poking her nephew's bare chest with her rough fingertip.

"Damn, girl. Pipe down. You gon' wake momma up. Calm yo' ass down," he urged.

"I was out with Lil Marc. See how much you know," he used his young, unsuspecting friend as an alibi.

"Yeah, well, you must had fell up in Joanne's ass right after that because I saw you leaving Ty's house this morning. Don't worry about it though. I'll take this money down the street. It's yo' loss." Crystal ended the useless chatter, seeing it was going nowhere.

Crystal turned her back to her nephew to walk away. Dirty stepped out the door and stopped her in her tracks.

"Here, Crystal, damn," he said digging into his socks.

"Take this money, Auntie," he only called her that when he needed a favor.

Crystal unraveled the bills and counted out sixty dollars. It was hush money. He began to suspect that his aunt had known about him and Joanne for months.

But Crystal would never rat out her own nephew under any condition. She knew the truth would send Tyrone flying over the edge, killing his fiancée and Dirty. She'd seen her brother lose all rationale over a woman before.

"Cryssy!" A voice screeched from the room opposite Dirty's.

"I'll holler at you, Twan. Momma calling me. I gotta go see what she wants."

Crystal opened the room door to see a frail, ailing woman that looked well past her age. She had given birth to the twins, Crystal and Clee, then Tyrone. She had been dying ever since her son's early departure, and she continued to get sicker as her daughter increased her daily worries.

"What you need, momma?" Crystal rushed to her mother's bedside.

"I just wanted to see what all the fuss was about. Y'all two stay keeping up some mess," Momma Hunter said.

"Oh, it ain't nothing. I was just telling Antwan to clean up that nasty room. You know how your grandson, Dirty is. That's why we call his roguish tail that," she rambled.

"Ma, you go on and get you some rest, I don't want you worrying about nothing," she kissed her mother on the forehead and headed for the door.

"Twan is in his room if you need something, Momma. I'll be right back. I gotta go run down the street to Monique's house. I love you."

Crystal left a crack in her mother's door and shot hastily towards her destination.

Chapter 4

Daddy's Throne

Tanisha sat across the street from home on her best friend Camiya's porch. They both sat in the cool of the spring evening, blowing their tiny cares in the wind.

Camiya was only fourteen but was granted much more freedom than her friend. Her mother knew that she smoked weed and allowed her to drink alcohol only in the confines of her home. It was the best parenting she could come up with after learning her daughter was doing so behind her back.

"Ta Ta, this not the same gas you had this morning. This one smoke way better. Where this come from?" she asked in her country accent.

"Dirty gave me this. I hit my momma stash for what we smoked earlier," Tanisha replied.

The mention of Dirty's name sprung pleasurable thoughts to Camiya's young adolescent mind. She saw his bold handsomeness and his clean-cut hair that he never went a week of missing a barber appointment for a touch-up. Those young, tight muscles on that lean body had her in entranced the most by far. Her young undeveloped body trembled in lust as if she'd caught a brisk icy breeze on the front porch.

"Ooh, Twan! Yo' fine ass cousin. You know I have been wanting to smash. I'm gone be yo' bestie and your cousin-in-law!" Camiya said excitedly, although, she hadn't engaged in sex yet.

"Shut up, Miya. You know good and well you a virgin still," Tanisha tried shooting down her friend's hopes of getting it on with her cousin.

"And pass the blunt. You sucking like your life depending on it," she added.

"So, you act like you ain't, though," Camiya said defensively.

"Ain't what?" Tanisha quizzed, looking confused.

"A virgin, Ta Ta. Never have you either. Yeah, like I thought," Camiya assured as the sound of her voice was muted by her friend.

Tanisha hit the weed, causing the fire to illuminate the obscurity of the dark porch. Her friend's comment had blown right over her head. She felt no pressure to fit in.

Sex was one conversation Camiya would have to settle for a loss in if Tanisha chose to engage. Luckily, Tanisha didn't feel slighted at that last assumption. Just as she exhaled the green monster, she noticed a dark colored Impala stop in the middle of the road.

"Who the fuck is that?" Camiya inquired first.

"I don't even know. Must be somebody for your mom."

"I doubt it. Because she ain't told me nothing," Camiya replied.

The car crept off slowly after a brief stall. Minutes later, Tanisha got a sight of what she'd been anticipating the past few days.

"There go Big Ty, your daddy!" Camiya spoke, reaching for the weed again.

"You know you better hand that over to the grown folk for you in be in the house for half the year." Camiya laughed.

The black two door CTS-V Cadillac coupe on black Lexani 22's pulled into the driveway next to Joanne's Ford Explorer. Tanisha immediately grabbed her small handbag in pursuit of her body spray and some candy mints. She knew it wouldn't be long before Tyrone yelled her name from the driveway if he noticed her.

Tyrone was overly protective of Tanisha. He knew that she was the prettiest cinnamon brown girl on the street and around the corner. And that wasn't just because he called her his daughter.

He was skeptical of Camiya, guessing she was progressive for her age. And having a stripper for a mother made things no better from his perspective.

On numerous occasions, he'd made it rain on Red Cherry in Raleigh's underground erotic scene. He'd even paid for one of her best private performances to date which she provided his crew of constituents.

The memories were vivid. Luckily, he never touched her to relieve himself of any unwanted drama. Routinely, he would quickly pull Tanisha away from the clutches of Red Cherry.

He stepped out, left leg, then right. Careful not to rip his delicate Armani linen. He stood up, brushing any would-be wrinkles from his black, button-down attire, then he shook his dress pants over his hard bottom shoes. His chunky yellow diamond bracelet dangled loosely on his muscular wrist.

Keys in hand, he reached onto the passenger side, emerging with a few gift bags. Tyrone looked around a couple of times, checking his surroundings. His conscience was not letting up from what he had just left behind prior to coming home.

Although well-known and respected, he also had to factor in the younger generation who didn't care the least and would do anything to solidify their own status in the world. Other than those that knew of his illicit affairs, the rest only took Tyrone for what he conveyed to the public, Quiet Storm's Tow and Recovery.

A Dodge Charger full of rowdy teenagers zooming past triggered the flashback of a blood riddled man's face. He reached underneath his seat, fearing they were a potential threat, out for vengeance.

The driver was a young female, along with a couple of male adolescents and another young, innocent teenage girl. They waved their hands into the air, vibing to the car's stereo as they turned the corner, past the stop sign.

Tyrone surmised the facts in his head. Besides Fat Boy and Munchie, no one else witnessed what he'd done. And Jip, he would only be able to explain his departure to the spirits.

Chapter 5

Ice Grill

The door of the house pulled open, and the screen door was pushed to accommodate Tyrone's entrance. Joanne's full, shapely figure stood in the doorway aroused by her man's arrival and what might be in the bags he was carrying. Tyrone stepped through the door, brushing past fiancée.

"Hey, baby," Ty greeted her.

Joanne turned away towards the couch and sat, crossing one brown thigh over the other. "Hey to you too," she replied in a nonchalant manner.

"Damn, baby, I know you missed your man," he smiled, promoting a full set of pearly whites, every tooth perfectly aligned.

"You know what? Yeen' got to show it though," Ty knew it was just a ploy for attention.

Joanne was trying her best not to get caught up in the maze of Tyrone's dark brown eyes. They were just as dizzying as the deep waves swirling in his hair. In addition to the hard body he possessed, the extras made things even more complicated.

Tyrone looked like he was cut straight from a page out of GQ Magazine. At just 29 years old, he was a lady killer. And Joanne's pretentious attitude didn't stand a chance much longer.

He stepped closer to his woman and placed the bags onto the floor. His Gucci cologne, Guilty, was driving her senses insane.

"I brought you a little something," he whispered near her ear, a scent of Cognac on his breath.

Tyrone kissed her gently on the neck, causing Joanne's body to tremble. She fell in love all over again at the slightest touch. It never took long for her to start missing his affection.

"Oh, yeah, baby!" she uttered as she spread her thick thighs, becoming moist.

"You always know the right things to do to get my pussy wet!" she said, caressing her man's upper back.

A rapid knock on the glass of the screen door broke the couple's moment of bliss, causing Tyrone to turn around.

"See, Daddy, we almost scared you," Tanisha giggled, stepping on the inside of the door.

"Y'all not scaring nothing. Come here, Princess!" he spread his strong solid arms. He embraced Tanisha tightly, giving her a kiss on the cheek.

"What's that I smell? I know it ain't weed," he pulled himself back to examine her tiny face.

"Man, easy unc'. I was blowing that gas before I walked in the crib. It got on Ta a lil bit, but she'll live," Dirty said with his right hand extended, waiting for Tyrone's hand.

Tanisha backed away, more than happy that she was saved by Dirty's quick thinking.

Tyrone clapped his right hand together with his nephew's and gave him a hug. Dirty's eyes were planted on Joanne who was now smoking a vape on the couch.

Dirty and Joanne were having a cold stare down. She quickly crossed one leg over the other and blew the lemon-flavored vapor in his direction. It was a clear sign of rejection now that her man was back home.

"Nigga, if you won't my brother, Clearance Clee's son, I'd kill you for talking like that," Ty threatened with a point of his index finger.

Tyrone wasn't smiling.

Dirty observed the abrasions on his knuckles, then he saw the rawness in his eyes. He knew that someone had to be on the receiving end of something ugly. Taking Tyrone's kindness for weakness he assumed. But then, it dawned on him. A name came to mind – Jip.

"So, what's good, Dirty?" Ty asked, trying to snap back into family mode.

Shit. Just waiting on you to get settled in so I can make something shake," Dirty responded.

"Ain't nothing wrong with that, family. Soon as I get my feet planted, we both good," Ty rubbed his palms together.

"So, daddy, what you got in the baggies?" Tanisha inquired anxiously.

"My bad, Princess. Here you go Ta. Can't come off the road empty handed with you on my mind, baby girl," Ty grinned.

Tanisha grabbed the black bag that Tyrone dangled in front of her. She dug her petite hand inside and emerged with a Jordan shoe box. She unveiled a pair of pink suede 4's, then jumped to hug her stepfather.

"I love these! And I got some fits to match these too! Thank you!" she said hugging him again to show her gratitude.

"What about me, daddy?" Joanne interrogated her man with a touch of envy.

Tanisha slid off into the seclusion of her room.

"I'll show you what I got for you in a minute, queen. It won't be long though, because papi need some R and R," Ty yawned showing some fatigue.

"Yea, yea, unc' I get the hints and shit. I'm about to go down here and check on momma anyway. Tomorrow, Friday so, I know we 'bout to be all gas no brakes," Dirty backed up for the door.

"Tell momma, I'll be down there in the morning, Twan. A nigga finna lay it down for now," Ty alluded.

Tyrone locked the latches behind his nephew and turned his attention towards Joanne.

"Meet me in the bedroom, sexy. You know your man don't get tired," Ty strained a smirk, although he really was exhausted.

"Well, you gonna be in a damn coma after I finish putting this pussy on you!" she twisted seductively to the bedroom.

Tyrone grabbed the bags from the couch and strutted behind, rubbing his tapered mustache and goatee. When it came to sex, he knew that

Joanne's lovemaking was extreme. There were no mediocre moments, making it easy for him to rise to the occasion every time.

Joanne had no patience for what was in the gift bags, though she knew it was probably lingerie. She pulled Tyrone by the collar into the bedroom and immediately unraveled his belt.

She threw her long tongue into his mouth and sucked on his wildly as she unbuttoned his shirt. She removed her tongue from his mouth and began licking his chest. She sucked on his nipples briefly, then proceeded further south.

Joanne wasted no time reaching for his swollen tip and constricting her mouth around it. She took him all the way in.

Tyrone felt his body melt into a trance that his lady's head game was sending him into. His right hand edged across the wall until his fingers found the light switch and flipped it off.

The headboard rammed and beat up the wall for two hours straight, causing turmoil for the young Tanisha. Her parents were a true contradiction that sex was something to hold out on, like she was warned of.

The only relief she could think of, was to turn up the volume on the Trey Songz and wonder how her next intimate encounter would be. Would she detest it due to the feeling of desecration or would it come from a more loving place this time?

Prey 4 Keeps

Chapter 6

Bait

Tyrone took off his black leather gloves. He wanted to feel the flesh smack up against the bare knuckles of his hands every time they collided with Jip's jaw.

Munchie and Fat Boy, both stood with their Louisville Sluggers in hand. They were anxiously awaiting their turns to get another crack at what used to be a set of perfectly functioning knees.

A terrified and swollen, Jip, sat in the wooden chair, legs and arms tied. He was helpless and stripped to his Suede Hyena boxer briefs in an abandoned chicken coop in the woods. He couldn't believe he had fell for the oldest trick in the game.

Sakeetha had never given Jip the time of day, even when he was dressed to impress and at his best. He knew that he was uglier than the Grinch Who Stole Christmas, so he flashed money as a baiting mechanism. But not even monetary status seemed to persuade her.

Suddenly, it seemed as if hell had frozen over and swine could fly. He went from the Grinch to Pretty Boy Floyd in only a matter of seconds.

"Damn, nigga! You don't fuck with me?" Sakeetha asked after seeing Jip hop out of the black H2 Hummer at the local store. He was purposely ignoring her, tired of his advances being shot down.

"Excuse me. What's that?" he played naïve, stopping in his tracks.

Jip approached Sakeetha's driver's side door. He aggressive advances immediately turned into a warm, womanly smile. She relaxed in the leather of her 2004 black Lexus 430.

"I know, I know. You thank I'm always trying to handle you. But see, you got to understand and realize I was fucking with that crazy ass nigga from Africa, and he say, we don't play bout our women where he from in Somalia," she waited for a reaction.

"Somalia! Gotdamn, girl. No wonder. Them niggas is crazy!"

"I'm trynna make it up to you though," Sakeetha implied as she batted her long, dark lashes enticingly.

Jip took a glance into the seat that she was sitting in. She had on a black one-piece mini skirt. It was rising up her thighs and she had no intentions of pulling it down to cover what was exposed. She was a red bone and, Jip was plum-crazy for the type. He was all ears.

"And how you plan on doing all that? That's a lot of patching up with all this hurt yo' fine ass gave me," he held his chest near his heart.

Jip wiggled his long sleeve Polo, causing his custom Rolex to dangle low on his wrist. He already had her in the bag but continued to show off a little.

"Come smoke something with me. My treat. Lemme cook you something to eat and see if you forgive me then," Sakeetha suggested.

"I'm with that, shawty. Let me grab a six pack of Coronas out this sto' and I'll be right out," he agreed to the invite.

As he followed, Sakeetha made sure to keep him in her rearview. She didn't want to lose him on this night. They ended up in a mobile home community, minutes from southeast Raleigh's city limits off of Barwell Rd.

Sakeetha sat in her car once she pulled up to the double wide mobile home. It was considered upscale in the mobile community, even better than a lot of houses in other areas of the city.

Jip stepped down from the H2 Hummer, wondering what could have been the hold up.

"Sakeetha, we going inside? We both country, but ain't trynna camp out in the woods," he cynically said.

Sakeetha was busy digging through her purse.

"Hold on, I'm trying to find where I put this damn weed at," she implied, sifting around the purse's contents.

Jip could hear the croaks of bullfrogs from the nearby creek. They all performed with each other in accordance, consecutively and simultaneously. The crickets chirped and added their own sound to the symphony.

"Gotdamn, them frogs louder than a mu'fucker. Aaggh!"

[ZZZGH! ZZZG! Z Z!]

Jip felt a powerful jolt of electricity conduce his entire nervous system he struggled, but only for a second.

"Aang, Aagh, Aah!" he grunted as he lay, shaking like a fish out of water. His mind could only access that he'd been played like a quarter in a broken-down arcade before he blacked out.

Munchie and Fat Boy hog tied Jip's hands and feet, then snatched him up from the ground. He took a ride in the rear of his own vehicle, unconscious, listening to the Rick Ross, Port of Miami album from his own playlist.

A bucket of ice-cold water splashed the comatose man's face. He awoke abruptly, gasping for air as if he were being drowned. Seconds after he opened his eyes, his blurry vision began to clear.

Tyrone smashed his knuckles once again into Jip's face. He hit the bridge of his nose, causing blood to spatter from the instant gash that opened. He snatched the brown bandanna from the inside of the hostage's mouth.

Jip sucked in as much air his lungs could hold. He spat blood onto the dirt floor of what used to house dozens of live chickens for slaughter. It would be the first time he was allowed to talk.

"Fuck you, Ty!" he spewed.

"See, that's crazy you would say that. Because that's exactly what you did to me when you ran off for months without paying for them two birds," Ty shook his head in disgust.

Sobbing profusely, Jip explained his sudden disappearance.

"Big Momma died, mane down in Atlanta. She ain't have no insurance. I had to pay for the funeral, mane."

"Yea, I know you did. That's why I came down to the A to pay my respects with you. But yo' granny must've had her funeral at the strip club. Cause that's sure as hell where I saw yo' fake ass trynna make it rain. You remember that?" Ty inquired.

"My grandma was young, bruh! She used to be a stripper in Magic City back in the day! She said that's how she wanted to be remembered. She said, make it rain, baby! Make it rain!" Jip continued to cry.

He figured he was about to lose the rest of his teeth, or worse, a limb.

Fat Boy laughed at Jip's dramatic antics, while Munchie held a solid ice-grill. The two were ready to put Jip out cold again, permanently.

"You used to be funny in school Jip. We stayed in Miss Taylor's in school suspension back at Ligon. I see you still got it. You stupid for coming back to Raleigh though. It was no problem for me to chase you down there. I had business to tend to. I found new territory to expand my Quiet Storm tow business," Ty said, making it known that it was worth the trip.

"I trusted you. But then again, that was asinine on my part to trust a nigga with a name like Jip," he said along with a backhand swing for punctuation.

Tyrone's 220 lb. frame sent Jip's out of shape body flying to the ground, still strapped to the chair.

Tyrone still had on his tailored linen, but careful not to tear or soil them with dirt or blood. He had to maintain that fresh from vacation look when he arrived home.

Jip yelled in distress but was quickly muffled by the bloody bandanna being plugged back into his mouth.

Munchie lifted the chair back up into an upright position. Fat Boy swung the bat at his right knee, then Munchie swung, fracturing his left.

Jip couldn't wait to get this over with so, he could kill Tyrone. After all, Tyrone wasn't young and dumb the way he remembered him from school. He was a businessman. Not a killer.

"Man, damn. I bet you never thought that one day you'd be on death row," Ty alluded.

Jip's eyes grew wide in suspense as he watched Tyrone reach into his pants pocket. He soon realized that his fate would be death by lethal injection.

Tyrone held 10cc's of cyanide in his right hand.

"You know what it means when that red light come on at Central Prison, right? Guns can be so messy sometimes, don't you agree? I'll say, it'll take me about thirty minutes to go freshen up, then fifteen to shoot down Poole Road, home to wifey. And another five minutes to get my dick wet. I'd say, you'd most likely be dead. Oh, and that bitch, Sakeetha. Fat Boy and Munchie about to run a train on that hoe," Ty added insult to injury.

Far from his old ways of doing things, Tyrone took what he thought to be a more reserved approach. He figured, if Jip had only considered his old reputation, he could've avoided an early grave.

Jip jerked his body sporadically in the chair, but to no avail. He was futile in his efforts as he begged for a miracle.

Munchie and Fat Boy held him firmly in their grasp. His veins protruded, revealing themselves to breached by the needle.

Tyrone removed the cap, then pushed the air out as he adjusted the syringe. A squirt of cyanide was dispersed from the tip. Jip had hoped that one little drop would keep him from checking out entirely.

The thin needle penetrated the vein, injecting the full 10 cubic centimeters. Tyrone held court in the backwoods. The syringe fell to the dirt floor empty, and Tyrone crushed it underneath his hard bottom shoe.

Jip's face began to look like he was choking on a chicken bone. He watched the three men exit from his sight. He said his final prayer and hoped it was received.

***

Tyrone sat straight up in his bed and wiped his forehead free of the drenching sweat. The nightmare was seeming to outlast his enemies. He had only wished it was a dramatic play in his mind. He looked over at his beautiful future, Joanne. She was still sleeping soundly.

The hypothetical scene was real. He looked down at his knuckles and ran his fingers across them. They were already beginning to scab.

He sat and thought to himself for a moment. The next time he went on vacation, it wouldn't be to track someone down. It would be a celebration of life.

Chapter 7

New Era

Moon's Cricket phone vibrated on the side of his hip. For a crack smoker, Moon had it going on compared to the addicts he knew. His phone stayed activated, courtesy of Tyrone. It was a flip phone for the ages.

Moon also wore more gold than a little bit. He loved sporting current and retro Nike jumpsuits with the old school Nike Cortez.

When Moon wasn't catering to his addiction, he was still sharpening his edge on young, unseasoned women. Sometimes, Dirty had to even compete, snatching the hot female prospects in the neighborhood before Moon caught wind of them.

"Man, O.G., turn that shit off! What type of smoker watches himself fuck on a homemade flick?" Dirty asked as he sat on the kitchen bar stool, puffing a vanilla rollup the size of a pinky.

Moon stopped texting his message in his phone. He directed his attention to his floor model television.

"Youngblood, that's classic shit right there. Adult Video Awards nomination, nineteen eighty-nine. Me in my prime." Moon shot a stern look as he took offense.

He got some type of a kick out of watching himself dominate the white man's woman on camera. Plus, it gave him the nostalgic feeling he yearned to be young again.

"Shit, I'm just fuckin' them, like they did our race hundreds of years. And another thang lil nigga. I'm mo' than just some smoker. You'll learn that one way or another. If you look down on most of yo' clientele that's less put together than me, you won't last long. Respect the motherfucka that's putting money in yo' pockets, regardless of how strung out they is," Moon dropped a few life lessons for Dirty to live by.

Although, Dirty knew Moon from the neighborhood and being around his uncle, Tyrone, he'd never had a proper introduction to the O.G. Addict or not, Moon expected nothing less than respect.

"That lil nigga still back there shittin'? He needs to flush 'cause I smell it. He gon' mold my momma walls," Moon contorted his nose, causing Dirty to laugh.

"Lil Marc, brang yo' ass outta there, nigga! He probably in there beatin' his meat, Moon. He don't get no pussy," Dirty clowned.

Moon's phone alerted him with a text.

"That's the President right there," he said, deleting the message.

"On the phone?"

"Nawl. At the doe," Moon replied.

Dirty jumped up from the bar stool and peeked through the blinds of the house's kitchen door.

"Damn, nigga. You peeking like you the candy lady. Open the doe!" Ty spat.

Tyrone stepped inside with a Jordan shoe box, swinging inside of a Foot Locker bag.

"Man, you know this ain't really M. J. shit in this bag," Ty spewed, clearly aggravated about something else.

"Awl, Hell nawl!" Ty said as he covered his eyes with his right arm.

"I should've known. You watch that shit at least twice a month, Moon. Man, anyway, O.G, I need your expertise on this," Ty said, ignoring the 80's model tv that surprisingly still worked perfectly.

Tyrone heard the bathroom toilet flush in the background and peeked towards the hallway.

"Who the hell back there?"

Dirty's friend, Lil Marc came out, massaging his stomach.

"Damn, that Frank's Pizza had a nigga stomach greasy," he said.

Tyrone looked at his Rolex. It was 10:15 a.m.

"Lil Marc, ain't you supposed to be in school? This the trap spot, not Ligon Middle youngin'!"

"I missed the bus," Lil Marc lied as he sat down on the couch.

"That's alright. I got a bus right outside with a Cadillac sign on it. I'm gonna make sho' you get to Lenoir Street. Go wait in the car," Ty commanded.

Dirty laughed in the background as Lil Marc walked out with his head down. Tyrone pushed the back of his head as he exited the screen door.

"Shit ain't funny, Dirty," Ty said aggressively.

"Okay. Let me see what you working with, Ty," Moon said grabbing the bag to look over its contents.

From the inside of the box, he retrieved a bag with a powder residue all over it's insides. He observed the texture of the cocaine that was in it. There were thirty-six ounces divided into eighteen bags.

"I'm 'bout to go check momma out for a minute and see how she is doing. Plus, I got to go back by the office to make sure the wifey got everythang under control. Dirty, you stick around with this ol' freak, he might teach you how to pull one of them seasoned hoes," Ty said in a humorous fashion.

The rhythm of Dirty's heart changed a beat. He was already covered in that area.

"Awl, talking to this young nigga is like pissing in the wind, nephew. Yella pee pee all on my Nike suit. But don't you worry about nothing. I got this. You know I'm gon' brang it back twice as fat like a Big Mac!" Moon assured his success.

Dirty laughed at the old school addict, amused that he was trapped in an expired era.

"Man, you need to get with this new century shit, Moon. That's why yo' ass still pulling them old freaks at the bingo parlor on South Saunders. Got Jehri curl activator juice fucking up yo' couch. Ont know why yeen got plastic covers on it. His ass must ain't get the memo we in year two thousand seven, unc," Dirty joked.

"You might have to stop back and make sho' ain't strangled yo' nephew, Ty!" Moon said with a straight face.

Tyrone stepped from the inside of Moon's weathered home, making his way to his two door Cadillac. A dark blue 2005 Impala with medium tint, crept by a little too slow for comfort. Four occupants glanced Tyrone's direction. He placed his hand on the hand of his gun, while approaching his car. Suddenly, the car accelerated its pace and disappeared around the corner.

"Who was that?" Lil Marc asked as Tyrone sat behind the wheel.

"I don't know. But anytime I catch your lil ass out here during school hours, I'm checking you in," Ty retorted.

Chapter 8

Knows Best

Mother Hunter's eyes grew wide at the sight of her only living son. Even though Tyrone's hands were involved in much of the city's underhandedness, which she was aware of, he was still her little boy.

Tyrone eased his way to the side of his mother's bed. He positioned her pillows to comfortably accommodate her better.

"Momma look. I bought your favorite – white roses," he laid the dozen flowers in her arms so she could smell and feel them.

"Remember, pops used to say you're too special for those same red roses everyone gave their wives. You used to say, all the dirt he did would just take a backseat anytime he gave them to you."

Mother Hunter grabbed Tyrone's youthful hands with her aged ones.

"How's Joanne doing, son?" she strained for her words to come out.

"She's fine, ma. A real good woman I got, just beautiful. She kind of reminds me of you," Ty replied.

"Of me? Well, you know, times have changed. The women these days just ain't the same as they used to be. Stood by their man through thick and thin. I think if they'd spend less time on that Bookface you could really get to know what the other got going on."

"Ma, trust me, she's one of the good ones, believe me," Ty assured without the least bit of doubt.

"Well, when you become my age, son, you start to sense thangs. My momma did the same in her old age. She said, it was hereditary, but who knows but the good Lord Jesus," Mother Hunter continued.

"A woman is only as good as what she let's a man see," she sighed.

Tyrone's mother stalled. She began to cough abruptly. He helped prop her up on her pillows and passed her a cup of water that sat on the nightstand next to her. She cuffed the glass and took a sip.

"Thank you, baby. It don't brang me joy to tell you this. But a terrible storm is coming. My knees giving me the signs, have mercy. Lightning striking somewhere close to home," she paused and coughed briefly again.

"Flood waters arising. Prepare like God told Noah 'fore he built the Arch that saved all life," Mother Hunter uttered as she stared at Tyrone with tired eyes.

Tyrone knew that his mother's days could be numbered. But he was at a loss with her state of mind.

"A terrible storm coming? It's sunny outside. And Joanne, I mean, she's had hard times, but she's a good woman. But you know, nobody's ever perfect from your momma's point of view," Ty told himself.

Tyrone would never disrespect or challenge his own mother.

In his mind, her poor health had to be playing a role in her choice of words. Altogether, he just assessed that, the woman who gave birth and raised him, had traveled a long hard road in her sixty years of living.

She watched her husband go to prison and lose his life in the system. Not once did she see another man before he died. She saw her oldest son, Clearance Clee Hunter, lose his life over drugs. And her daughter, Crystal was the biggest surprise, after all the time they spent in the church together, paying tithes and giving praise. But luckily, she stayed steadfast herself in case there was hell to pay for those who didn't.

Tyrone turned around to see his sister, Crystal standing at the door. He arose from his bent position and wiped what was not yet a fully developed tear from the corner of his eye.

Crystal walked over and put her right hand on her younger brother's shoulder.

"You go on ahead, baby brother. I got her," she said.

Tyrone hugged, then looked into Crystal's eyes, still holding on.

"How you doing, Cryssy? You still holding strong and staying clean?"

"Yeah, bro. Twelve weeks strong and counting," the lie crossed between two missing teeth.

"That's good, sis. I'm proud of you, really. Hey Cryssy, look. I know I ain't been no saint so, I can't preach, but I promise we gonna get this family – "

"It's okay, Ty. We'll be okay," Crystal stopped her brother from finishing his sentence. She knew that he was feeling the pressure of fulfilling what his father never got a chance to do.

"Okay, I'll talk to you later, then. Love you, Crystal," Ty said, breaking his hold.

Tyrone headed for the door, feeling guilty for not spending more time with his mother, who only lived right down the block. The fact that he made a living off the same thing that had destroyed Crystal's teeth didn't sit well with him either.

Submerged in the wellbeing of his mother, Tyrone failed to notice the outside was now being battered by heavy rain. Water was rushing into the gutters, while yards were being puddled. The premonitions Mrs. Hunter had just promised replayed over again in Tyrone's head.

"Nawl, come on Ty. You know how superstitious these women in the south is," he blew off the assumption his mother was a psychic.

Chapter 9

Body-talk

"Jo Jo, you held a black man down something lovely these past few calendars. You kept a brother clicking his card at the commissary. And those flicks! Mmh! Good Law'd have mercy! The chaplain couldn't preach my dick to be a good boy. Baby, I stayed on swole!"

"I knew you would love 'em boo. You see my ass had got thicker too while you was in there?"

"Mmmh, hmm! Girl, you ain't never lied. That grown woman spread done kicked in real nice."

"I'm working on my abs, and trying to get my glutes right, too. But you know this ass ain't going nowhere. It's gon' remain phat, best believe."

"Aah, you funny, baby. Talking about glutes and shit! What you know about that? We stay on that type of time behind the wall. Muscle Men's magazines, protein this, protein that. Eating tunas straight out the pack and shit," the voice chuckled.

"You know what I was wondering though, baby?"

"What was you wondering? You know you don't have to wonder."

"Well, ever since I first seen that first ass-shot you sent me in the USP," he paused.

"You know, the one with you in that hot pink thong? I was asking myself, well, if, say, uh, if I put my face in that ass, could you make yo' booty clap on my face? I'm just saying, damn!"

"Baby, you don' got crazy silly, but I swear you always been a fool though. Got my pussy all hot!"

"Oh, yea! Hot and wet?"

"Yep. Hot and wet."

"I see that mouth still gets you in trouble. You make me wanna do some of the nastiest thangs to you, girl. I been working out, hitting the weights hard as hell. You think you can hang?"

"Oh, most definitely. I got my endurance, stamina up, all that good stuff. The question is, can you hang?"

"Well, is a pig's pussy poke? A giraffe's pussy high ain't it? But check this out, baby. You know, shit got put on hold due to my lil prison bid. But Daddy's home now," the demeanor of the voice stiffened.

"I'm ready to make that happen, you dig? I know by now this weak nigga weight gotta be up. I wanna catch his ass before he finally decides to move yo' exotic ass out of Raleigh to Florida somewhere."

"Well, baby, I'm still getting to that."

"What? What you mean, getting to that? I ain't got no patience to be playing games, Jo Jo! My mouth's been watering 'bout this come up my whole bid."

"I know, I know. Hold on, somebody's on the business line. Quiet Storm Tow and Recovery!"

"My old school sitting off Rush Street by the train tracks! I need it pulled 'fore one these roguish ass niggas snatch my shit and my babies!"

"Yo' babies?"

"My twenty eights, damn! Done fucked up my Friday!"

"Okay, what's wrong with it?"

"Ont know. It just knocked off on me."

"I hate it for you, but lemme get one of our guys out there before you have a fit. It'll get a diagnostics test. We on the way, just hold tight."

"Okay, I'm back. Look, we gonna handle that. Shit!"

"Shit what?"

"I gotta go! I think he here!"

Tyrone stepped through the door, car keys dangling in hand. His Ralph Lauren plaid button down and black denim were just now beginning to dry since the rain his mother predicted had stopped.

Joanne ended her cell phone conversation and smiled at her fiancée.

"That was Tanisha. She said, don't worry about picking her up from Camiya's aunt's house later on. They're going to the skating rink for the weekend," she fabricated a bit.

Tanisha did call, but it was thirty minutes ago, prior to Tyrone's entrance. Her deceitfulness was void of any holes which made her feel a little turned on even.

Joanne knew this moment would come. She would have to make a choice that hadn't plagued her brain for the past three years. She knew now that it was no turning back. One lie would have to follow another, and she would have to be quick on her toes, in a mental sense.

"That's good, Ta Ta called and let you know. She can be a little grown sometimes. I was checking in on you, baby, seeing if I was overworking you."

Tyrone walked over to the chair where Joanne sat behind the desk and kissed her cheek affectionately.

"You so gorgeous!" he said, stepping back for a quick examination.

"I got to run down to this truck company then, back down to Moon crib. I got these new wreckers coming in. You need anything?" Ty asked.

Joanne looked a little tense.

"Nope. I'm good. You go right on ahead. I can send Kyrell across the street to get me something to eat," she said with an attitude.

Joanne grabbed the remote from the desk and flipped on the wall mounted flatscreen to VH1. The Love and Hip-Hop Atlanta marathon was on.

"Oh, that's how you do? Just flip it to Steebie J while I'm trying to show concern for my woman?" Ty spat.

Joanne folded her arms over her breast and looked at Tyrone sternly.

"What's down at Moon's house that can't wait? Some bitches? I heard about his old nasty ass."

"You know what's down there, Anne, stop playing. Don't no birds be over there, if that's what you so uptight about. Not the ones you talking 'bout."

"Yea, alright. I was just checking to see who was getting more devotion than me, which I thought a fiancée had rights to."

"My devotion? Okay. We'll talk about this later. I got business to attend to. I'm gone," Ty turned and pushed through the office door hastily.

"Bye, nigga. Lately, you ain't been 'round much these days noways," Joanne retorted in her newly broken language. Raleigh was gradually chopping away at her Detroit dialect.

Joanne scrolled down her phone and touched the last recent call. Tears were in her eyes and dark trails were on her cheeks from her eyeliner.

"Can you hear me?" she mumbled lowly through the speaker.

"I'm all ears, baby. It sounds like you fixin' to talk my language," the voice said.

***

Around the corner from his home, Tyrone stepped into Moon's place, through the kitchen door. The air reeked of high-grade weed burning, mixed with that of the Old Bay seafood battered chicken wings.

"Ty Hunter, what up, cutty," Sa'von greeted from the couch he and his cousin, Dirty sat on.

The two were playing NBA Live on the Xbox. It was the version with the rebirth of Micheal Jordan gracing the cover.

Sa'von was a first cousin of Tyrone's, and Dirty's second cousin. He was also an up-and-coming rapper, buzzing locally and on social media platforms.

"What up, Young Sanity? You good?" Ty slapped hands with the 17-year-old prospect.

"You heard from Fat Boy?"

"Yea, I seen him and Munchie. He told me to tell you to put him something to the side." Sa'von conveyed.

"Come to the stove, nephew. You hungry, nephew? I battered and fried them wangs myself, nephew," Moon handed Tyrone two pieces in a paper towel.

"I took care of that, nephew. You know I had me a taste, nephew. You know how I do. Nephew, that's some good shit, nephew!" Moon kept smacking his lips as if he'd just ate a McDonald's McRib.

Tyrone could tell that the cook-up had put Moon on the Moon. Whenever he was gone off a good batch, he'd call him nephew repeatedly.

Moon picked up a crushed Miller can. He moved around some cigarette ashes on top of it, then he proceeded to strike his Bic lighter. He tried to keep his cool demeanor.

Crack ruined families, like the twins, Crystal and Clee. It left babies with birth defects and learning disabilities. Fathers and mothers deprived and neglected their own children. Even the hustlers that once thrived off the money from it, received lifelong prison sentences in many cases.

The effects were innumerable. And for that reason, Tyrone wanted out soon.

Moon blew out the rest of the death-fog from what his lungs didn't consume.

"Anytime, nephew. Unc, gonna get it right fo' you."

Tyrone retrieved a digital scale from the cabinet and sat it on the countertop. He pushed the button, and a blue light illuminated. He placed a few bags on the silver plate. Each one on average was 10 grams less than double. After a few minutes, he walked over to where Dirty and Sa'von were thumbing the Xbox controllers.

"This is y'all right here. Take this nine, Dirt. You and Sane straight down the middle," Ty spoke to Dirty specifically.

"Y'all good with that?"

"Yea, we straight. Ty, handle your biz," Sa'von retorted.

Tyrone stepped back into the kitchen. He grabbed two bags of uncooked powder and tucked them inside his underwear. Moon was still flicking his lighter to the top of the can.

Tyrone reached for the kitchen door, then stopped. He turned and faced his nephew.

"Take Mike to the hole."

He wasn't talking about the video game. It was a metaphor for stashing the Foot Locker bag outside of the house.

"I got you, Ty. You see what D. Wade's work like," Dirty said as he crossed up Jordan with Miami Heat's future Hall of Famer.

Chapter 10

Blue Nights

Fetish, formerly known as Four Squares, was positioned across the street from Heritage Park in downtown Raleigh. A modest-sized strip club with one drink bar, that drew the after-hours crowd.

Only the ones who could afford to ball got off of the bench. Those with short money, sipping and not tipping, got kindly escorted out by the nearly 300lb security guards.

Blue Bull, Bandanna Smurf, and Clutch, sat on a long, tan, leather couch. Individually, neither of the three were the ballers that they portrayed or wanted to be even.

They were common crooks, making moves here and there, nothing consistent. Even the money that they threw in unison couldn't account for what the big tippers could dish out on their own.

Blue Bull tossed back his double shot of Crown Royal. He stood up in his white Dodgers coat and made his way towards the stage. He pulled a brick of one-dollar bills from the inside of his coat. Intimidated, an older guy in a tailor fitted suit, retreated to a table after sticking a 100-dollar bill in a dancer's stocking.

Blue Bull immediately began to paddle the first president's face from the top of the stack, onto the stripper's naked body. The blond-haired, caramel seductress was making her cheeks clap to the throw-back track, Pussy Poppin' by Ludacris. She could out clap a Sunday morning church choir. Bandanna Smurf and Clutch watched the show from a distance on the couch, while Blue Bull had his fun.

"Cuh, that lil bitch alright, but let me see what hit the stage next. You know, Bull love them light-skinned hoes. But me, I can't stand 'em," Smurf told Clutch with a distasteful look on his face.

"Man, what you got against the light skin broads. You don't ever tip, like you don't wanna show 'em no love," Clutch grimaced, displaying his diamond teeth.

"What's the history? I know it gotta be a story behind it."

"Facts. Facts. Man, some years back I had the finest brightest thang. I was wide the fuck open off this bitch like my nostrils when I used to be on that powder. But one day, this rapping ass nigga came through the Bull City," Smurf told it like it was yesterday.

Clutch could hear the violin begin to play in the background from the sob story.

"What was his name?" Clutch quizzed.

"DG Egg Yoke or Yoba. Some shit like that," Smurf tried recollecting.

"You mean, DG Yola?"

"Yea, that's it! You heard of 'em?" Smurf questioned.

"Yea, I ain't gon' let up and let them haters get to me, or some shit. That shit bang in the club, though," Clutch ran the beat through his memory.

"So, what happened?" he asked.

"That nigga scooped my young tender thang. I ain't seen that bitch since. They say she ran down to ATL or Miami. You know how these hoes do," Smurf said as if he was hurt emotionally.

"So, what the hell light-skin got to do with that? Nigga, you trippin'." Clutch asserted.

"Nawl, ain't trippin'. That shit sent me into post traumatic syndrome," Smurf replied shamefully.

"Man, you dramatic. One girl fucked you up like that. You weak." Clutch implied.

"My brother told me, them high yella chicks get you kool points when you young. But when they get older, they show they true colors. They start actin' up when they find out every nigga in the NBA want 'em.

"Here, have a drank on me, Smurf."

Clutch smacked a half-naked waitress on the ass. She was walking with a tray full of drinks.

The pretty bottle lady turned around swiftly. She was angry until she caught an eyeful of the gangster's physical attributes.

Clutch wore a white Polo Ralp Lauren with a big orange horse and jockey on it. It was sort of fitted to his frame, around his muscular build, showcasing his biceps.

"Let me get two of them Hennessy shots. Make 'em both a double. Keep the change, sweetie."

The money eased the humiliation she felt.

Clutch handed her a crispy 50-dollar bill. He took photo shots with his eyes of the 5' 6, green-eyed, mocha cream toned bombshell.

Her hair was cut short and kept in a Meagon Good type of manner. Her breast and other assets were covered up except for her flat stomach and lower thighs. She was draped in purple with trims of pink in her ensemble. Even her toes were painted to match.

"Sure thang. I'll be right back," she said in her southern twang.

Clutch sat up properly as she returned. His mind was no longer concerned with the drinks.

"Thank you, Miss. Sorry about slapping your ass like that. That wasn't nice. You dancing tonight?"

"Apology accepted. I just do dranks, boo. My homegirl, Cherry got me this job. She needed me to watch her back."

Bandanna Smurf's eyes lit up at the mention of the name, Cherry. He mumbled under the loud music pounding from the speakers.

"Nawl, can't be," he said, waving off the silly thought in his mind. He took a swig of the Hennessy.

Blue Bull was retracting away from the stage with sweat beads at the top of his forehead.

"My nigga, that's a nasty lil red-bone bitch! I got to have 'er!" Blue Bull said as he slapped Bandanna Smurf's hand. He could barely be heard as he hollered over the roll call.

The voice of DJ Dezerk came over the microphone, announcing the last performer. He told the nearly packed house what to brace themselves for.

"Okay, Raleigh! Y'all got y'all appetites wet a lil bit. But I know if you know what's good fo' ya, you saved some room for this next treat. The icing on the cake looks so sweet! And you know it's moist on the inside! But sitting right at the tippity top, is the main course of the night, RED-CHERRRY! I know you gonna wanna eat this fruit!"

DJ Dezerk quickly pushed the mic to the side.

"Man, who wrote this wack intro? I know you wanna eat this fruit. Gimme my check," he told the club owner standing next to him.

"Here she come," the waitress said, tapping Clutch on his shoulder.

The curtains were pulled back to the side by two white masked men in slacks and suspenders. It added to the dynamics for a more dramatic entrance.

Red Cherry rolled out onto the stage on a small, automated platform, filled with whip cream, strawberries, and cherries. Bandanna Smurf's eyes nearly popped out of his head.

"Oh, shit! Cherry!" Smurf loosened up the white flag he had tied around his neck. He'd already begun to sweat.

Red Cherry kneeled and turned around, doggystyle position. She ripped her sheer white skirt off with just one hand and pulled her red thong to the side.

Her shaved pussy lips stood out like a peach seed. She began to tighten her stomach muscles and commenced to push as if she was about to give birth.

She pushed on continuously until loads of whip cream came oozing from her love canal. It looked as if she had been gangbanged by five convicts, fresh from five years of unreleased tension.

After the final drop of cream, she gave one final push. A stem emerged. She turned around and pointed towards Smurf.

"You, come here," she signaled.

Bandanna Smurf tried to play it cool as he moved in closer. He was rushing on the inside.

"Pull it out, baby," she whispered with her lips as she made some extreme sex faces.

He did as he was told.

A dripping wet, red cherry popped out from between her walls. Cherry turned around, facing her participant of the night. She grabbed the berry by the stem.

Sticking her tongue out, she laid it on top. She sucked it, swallowed it, and spit out the stem. Smurf nearly ejaculated in his pants.

"So, what's your name, Miss Thang?" Clutch said as he took his eyes off the stage show.

"No, it's not, Miss Thang. It's Alexus," she corrected him.

Clutch threw his hands up in surrender.

"Okay, then. Alexus it is. I don't want no trouble," he put his hands back onto the table.

"So, what will the beautiful Alexus be doing after she's finished watch-dogging her friend?"

"Well, tonight we gonna leave together. I'm staying at her house so she can do my hair in the morning. I have something important lined up."

"I see. Well, I ain't trying to stop nothing. But I do want to get better acquainted with you," Clutch implied.

Red Cherry came strutting over in heels and a thong, her mango shaped breast bouncing.

Look, if you came with him, right there -"

She eyeballed Bandanna Smurf up and down, rubbing her burgundy weave.

"Y'all can continue this conversation at my house," Cherry suggested. She turned away and sat next to Bandanna Smurf.

Blue Bull walked over with a winning look on his face.

"Y'all go on 'head. I got a date with Bambi! All I need is the pipe from the whip and I'm good," Blue Bull told his team.

Bandanna Smurf turned and sat his sights on the pierced brown nipples of the lady sitting to his right.

"Cherry, you know a nigga missed that – "

"Shhh," she pressed his lips with her index finger, then stuck her tongue onto his earlobe.

"Save yo' breath. We got a lot of catching up to do."

Chapter 11

Rough House

Cherry's tongue was driving Bandanna Smurf up the walls of her dungeon. She had a pink vibrator plugged in her ass and his nine inches in her mouth. The two orange swan x pills had her sex game in overdrive as she rekindled her flame with an old sponsor.

Bandanna Smurf pulled himself from stroking her warm throat and got ready for a dive in her deep canal without a wetsuit. Like the Ol' Dirty Bastard sang before his passing; he liked it raw.

It wasn't a race. He slid inside Ref Cherry's thick, juicy tunnel at a timid pace. Once inside, Smurf felt her red nails claw into his back. He began pounding away at her guts. His intentions were to punish her for the disappearing act she pulled while he was in love with her.

Red Cherry cried and moaned for more of a thrashing as he jabbed her insides like a jackhammer. She took on the challenge of seeing who could outdo the other. She pushed him off of her onto his back and straddled him backwards. She pounded her 44-inch waist onto his pelvis repeatedly.

Bandanna Smurf was no more than 5 feet 6 inches, 165 lbs. His bones were being pressure tested by the 29-year-old sex fiend. He tried to man up, but her insides were too wet, too sloppy, and too warm to keep a secret.

"Ahh! Ohh!" Smurf's thoughts escaped his mind and leaped out of his mouth. His excited reactions traveled from the bedroom to the living room.

"Ha ha! Oh my God!" Alexus laughed, pointing a finger at Clutch.

"Your boy is off the chain! He better control that donkey. My girl must be in there killin' his ass. He shouting like he in church."

"Must be nice. Shit, I wanna yell like my boy too. Take me to church, Lord."

Clutch grinned. Alexus smirked. He went in to kiss her on her earlobe. She moaned. He sucked her neck. She tilted her head back. His hand traveled underneath her skirt. She pushed him away.

"Look, I know you heard this before, but I don't usually fuck on the first night. On the other hand, ain't had sex in nine months today. So, this better be good," Alexus strongly advised.

Alexus pulled out a Lifestyle condom. Clutch pulled out a gold package of his own.

"Okay then," Alexus said.

Bandanna Smurf was releasing all of the animosity he had built up over the years for Red Cherry. He slapped her gyrating cheeks, leaving them bruised with several palm prints.

Red Cherry had to force her head sideways a few times to avoid being suffocated. Smurf was drilling her from the back with his hands pushing her face into the pillow. She knew why he was being so rough, but she didn't care. The more pain, the more pleasure, the better the orgasm.

"Fuck me! Fuck me harder muthafucka! Yeen did shit like talking 'bout it!" Cherry taunted.

Red Cherry felt as if she had to pee. He was hitting her G-spot in spurts.

Bandanna Smurf took her taunts unkindly. He pulled the pink vibrator from her ass and spit onto his manhood. He thrusted it into her warm hole causing Red Cherry to ram her face into the pillow. She was in submission as he clenched his teeth and growled like a wild wolf.

Alexus slid up and down on top of Clutch like the horses on the carousel. She rode him as they both sat upright face to face, staring into each other's eyes. They were locked and synched. Her natural greens to his dark ones.

"Damn, baby," he whined.

Clutch couldn't believe that sex could be this good with a condom on. They felt so connected that he had to check to make sure the Magnum was still in place. The fact that he was also taking his time and making love was also blowing his mind.

She worked in a strip club, but didn't strip. He offered her a blue dolphin, she didn't pop. She was beautiful on the exterior, but maybe a freak on the inside. All of these unanswered thoughts in his mind. He thrusted his tongue into her mouth and passionately kissed away.

Clutch tried pounding her insides. She made him go slow. Maybe, trying to maintain some level of dignity. He hated slow grinding but loved slow grinding in Alexus.

Bandanna Smurf power-drived himself into Red Cherry's asshole. He was on edge and couldn't hold out any longer. He pulled his ass-stained pipe out.

"Turn yo' ass around!" he said aggressively as if he wanted to look his enemy in the eyes before sending him to hell.

Red Cherry faced his swollen manhood, panting heavily for air. Smurf pushed himself into her mouth. With no restraints, he pumped her face the same way he did her ass when he was hitting it from the back.

Red Cherry slobbed and sucked him like a Hoover vacuum. Her head bobbed back and forth until she felt him grip the back of her wig steady.

Bandanna Smurf shot his load into her throat until she nearly vomited from the immense amount.

"Bitch!" he grunted, finally feeling vindicated.

***

Clutch finally had Alexus the way he wanted. Face down, ass up. She held onto the couch arm as he beat her insides up from the back.

"Cum for me, baby!" she begged.

It turned him on to hear her whine. That was all he needed to hear. He pounded away until she whined even more. He and she both orgasmed simultaneously.

***

"Damn, nigga. I can see that you like to hold grudges. I'm sorry." Red Cherry spoke to break the monotony.

"Nawl, own't hold grudges. I kill 'em," Smurf retorted.

"Well, I hope ain't on that hitlist," Cherry said, searching his soulless eyes.

"On't know. Let me think about it," Smurf said sarcastically.

"Anyway, nigga. Do me a favor tomorrow," she said.

"Depends on what that is."

Bandanna Smurf wasn't letting up. He knew Red Cherry could easily have him wrapped around her finger if he wasn't careful.

"My Yukon is at my neighbor, Ty's shop. I need you to take me to pick it up."

A light bulb flickered on the inside of Bandanna Smurf's head.

"You said, Ty?" he beamed in.

"Yea. You know him?" Cherry quizzed.

"Scribe him fo' me."

"Kind of tall. Muscular, brown skin with deep waves. Clean cut, Sean Jean type of nigga," Cherry detailed Tyrone without discretion.

"Oh, nawl. That ain't him. I thought it was my man from the Bull City. He a light complexion with dreads," Smurf lied.

Bandanna Smurf and Clutch had been too high and drunk to notice where they were. Maybe, they came in the neighborhood from a different direction he thought. Whatever the case was, they'd unknowingly just landed even closer to their mark.

Tyrone could now be tracked from every angle. Bandanna Smurf's obsession with strip clubs and Red Cherry had paid off. No more riding through in the blue Impala like they'd driven the past week. They could plot their next move from inside. That's if Smurf played his cards right with Red Cherry.

"Okay, damn him. My truck. In the afternoon. You gonna take me or do I have to catch a Universal cab?" Cherry asked bluntly.

"Yea, I got you. Least I can do, after that fire ass pussy and head you gave me," Smurf thought he was funny.

Red Cherry felt the insult.

Smurf stood up and walked quietly into the living room in his boxers. He didn't want to block his friend from having a night as good as his.

Clutch had Alexus wrapped up in his muscular arms. He was watching Baby Boy on BET, while she was sleeping.

Bandanna Smurf put his fist to his mouth to contain his laughter.

"Loverboy ass nigga," he whispered as Clutch heard the floor crack.

"Come here nigga," Smurf signaled.

Clutch slid from underneath Alexus. The two friends crept into the kitchen.

"Check this out. The boy we are scoping out, he stays right 'cross the street," Smurf whispered.

"How you figure that?" Clutch asked.

"Ol' girl said she had to pick up her truck from her neighbor, Ty's shop. I checked the blinds and seen his whip myself."

"Shit. Good thang we rode out in the Beemer. We gotta give that Impala a rest," Clutch suggested.

"Yea, you right. I'm gon' just play the field a lil bit. See what we see," Smurf replied.

"See, now you talkin'. I'm about to fall back on this couch and beat this pussy up again. Alexus got that come-back," Clutch schemed.

"I'm 'bout to do the same shit to this no-good ass hoe back there. I owe her ass," Smurf pounded his fist into his palm.

"Damn, you need therapy, black man." Clutch shook his head in disbelief.

Chapter 12

Rotten

The alarm woke Tyrone from the comfort of his king-sized bed at 7 a.m. sharp. The Saturday morning sun was beaming in on his face, Joanne's 42-inch waist was snug up against his pelvis.

He eased himself up and studied his lady's beautiful face, her silky hair, and her bronze skin. In just her pink and black bra and thong set, he knew he'd never make his runs, plus, work on time if he stared too long.

Just two hours ago, they'd had wakeup sex. And at one in the morning, they'd had knock-out-cold sex.

All that Tyrone wanted in a woman; he could see in Joanne. Loyalty, love, and companionship was the key. He even wanted to have a child with her one day but believed it be best to wait until he wasn't straddling the fence between corporate and streets.

Tyrone's own father got sentenced to 30 years for a heroin conspiracy. Some high-priced federal lawyer, grandson to the Klans Grand-Dragon, deviously auctioned him off to a racist 4th Circuit federal judge.

Tyrone was 12 years old. His father, Thomas Hunter died of a stroke in the Leavenworth, Kansas U.S. Penitentiary by the time Tyrone was 19.

Joanne felt the bed shift. She turned around, facing her deep-in-thought fiancée. She stretched, then yawned.

"What's wrong, baby?" she inquired.

"Nothing, Anne," he downplayed.

"Tell me," Joanne was persistent.

"Just thinking about my Pops. How he went to prison, trying to solidify a future for his family, and died for it," Ty responded.

"Oh, baby," Joanne sighed and rubbed his face.

"He was a real father. Not like the rest of these sorry ass men. But don't worry. That won't be your fate. We gonna get married and have some kids. We can get to that tonight," she wrapped her left arm around Tyrone.

"I don't know, Anne. I want to be here for 'em," Ty had to differ.

Joanne removed her arm and sat upright on the bed.

"What? So, I'm good enough to fuckin' nut up in, lay-up, and play housewife, but not to have your kids?" Joanne spat.

"Nah, baby. You going too far. Did I say that? We gon' get married. The kids gonna happen. But now's not the time."

Tyrone slid from underneath the cover in his boxers. His 220 lb frame, bulging due to his workout routine and eating habits.

Joanne folded her arms, like a mad, little girl that couldn't get what she wanted. Insidious thoughts began to circulate within the confines of her mind.

"It's another bitch. That's why he stays using he's out of town so much as an excuse. That's okay. I know you don't love me."

Tyrone let her have her moment, seeing that she needed to cool down. He walked over to this cherry wood dresser and pulled open a drawer. He removed bundles of money wrapped in rubber bands from the inside. He carried them to the extended closet where his safe lied behind the wall.

Joanne waited until he stepped inside, then she entered in behind him. She grabbed a pair of high heels from the shelf as her reason for being in the same space.

Tyrone had his hidden safe door open. His woman probed its contents. Not since Detroit had she seen so much money crammed in one place. He looked over his shoulder, tossed a few money rolls inside, and secured the safe.

Joanne kneeled down and kissed him on the cheek.

"I'm sorry, baby. I ain't mean to make you upset. We can take our time. I'm more understanding than that," she admitted.

Tyrone turned to face her and the two embraced. They both stood up.

"I love you, Anne."

"I love you more," Joanne promised, pinching Tyrone's fat-free abs.

"I'm about to take a shower. Can you cook something?" Ty asked.

"Most definitely," Joanne emphasized.

Tyrone turned on the massaging shower heads. He palmed his African herbal soap bar and soiled his rag.

Joanne opened the refrigerator. She grabbed the eggs, cheese, onions, green peppers. Omelets were her morning specialty, along with the blueberry Belgian waffles she was about to prepare. Her newly acquired smartphone vibrated abruptly.

"Probably Ta Ta calling from this number. Always letting her phone die. Tanisha."

"Hey, darling. Good mawnin'!"

"Hey," Joanne replied dryly. Her eyes darted around the kitchen, in fear of Tyrone appearing.

"What are you cooking?"

"How you know I'm cooking?"

"Because I know you way better than he do.'"

The voice became stern.

"Let me ask you a more critical question. How long am I going to have to wait for my back to be scratched?"

"Not long. But you called at a bad time."

"So, why'd you answer the phone? Is it because you love me? Did you really think it was Ta Ta? How is my princess doing?"

Joanne stalled.

"Baby, we gon' make this happen, but I gotta go," she ended the call.

"Fuck!" the caller cursed in frustration and threw the phone to the floor.

***

From across the street, Bandanna Smurf and Clutch sat in the living room playing Casino, a common jailhouse card game. Clutch threw down a deuce of spades onto a five of spades.

"Build seven, tender dick," he called out.

Bandanna Smurf sighed. He didn't have a seven in either suit to pick up the cards with. He threw out a four of hearts. Clutch retrieved the deuce and the five with his seven of diamonds.

Smurf picked up the four of hearts with a spade four. He turned to look towards the living room blinds which he could see from the kitchen.

"She still cooking in her panties, creep ass nigga?" Clutch asked, throwing out his third card, an Ace of diamonds.

Smurf threw out a King of spades. He shook his head in disbelief that he had no card to collect the Ace for the 1 point.

"I can't see as good no mo'. She got that light off now," Smurf said, turning back towards the coffee table.

"Let's keep slanging these cards. Patience is a virtue my boy," Clutch assured.

Red Cherry was wrapping foil and highlighting blonde streaks into her friend's hair. Alexus sat under her care as she styled and gossiped the many details of the night away in the kitchen.

"Big! I mean, Mandigo, girl!" Cherry exclaimed as Alexus laughed.

"What was Clutch's like?"

"Girl, what you mean?" How would I know?" Alexus played hardball.

"Bitch, stop playing. I know better than that. You glowing, shining, and blang blangin', all in one!" Cherry shot back.

Alexus let down her guard reluctantly.

"He was gentle."

"Gentle? Them gangsta ass niggas? Smurf act like he ain't had no pussy since he came out of one."

Red Cherry was sure that her friend had to be talking about a different group of men.

"Well, they hang together, but I'm sorry, they are not the same," Alexus responded defensively.

"Anyway, that was just a one-time thang. I got my mind on going to this wedding. He can go right back to gang banging or whatever the hell it is they do," she said confidently.

"Look, check the boy out." Smurf threw down his cards.

Clutch jumped up from his seat.

"I told you. That's our man, right there," Smurf mumbled.

Tyrone opened the door of his Cadillac. Joanne was standing at the screen door in her rose-colored robe, her arms folded. He slowly backed out of the driveway, he turned right, then disappeared out of sight. Joanne closed the door.

"Damn, that nigga got a bad bitch!" Smurf groped himself.

"Man, focus sometimes, nigga."

"Man, I do. I wonder where he headed now, Mister Clutch?"

"Either, his car shop, 'cause most shops be open on Saturdays too. Or to make some moves probably. But once we find where this shop at, we can keep tabs on this fool from there too," Clutch said as he rubbed his palms together.

Chapter 13

Laundry Money

Tyrone sat in the office of his Quiet Storm's Tow and Recovery establishment. He was tallying up all of his employee's pay-sheets for the coming payday on Monday.

Whenever he was out of the office for the day, Joanne would usually fill in and handle the paperwork. The downside was the loose ends he had to tie up that she left behind.

"Looks like being a boss takes talent, cousin. You look frustrated over there at the desk. You supposed to have yo' feet up," Fat Boy said, sitting in his Quiet Storm uniform.

"Yea, all money ain't easy money, Fat. One day this going to keep all our black asses out of prison, though. Me, you, Sa'von, Dirty," Ty insinuated.

"I feel you, Ty. But what you need to do is, go and invest in Young Sanity with me. He 'bout to put the city on the map like it's supposed to be with this rap shit. We can be like Birdman 'n' Slim," the old Jay and Dame.

"That's something to thank about, Fat. I know cousin got a lil street fame, and the people gon' vouch," Ty said, rubbing his goatee.

"Meantime, what's up with that Kung Fu flick?" he asked.

"Oh, Bruce Lee was kicking harder than a mu'fucka. He need mo' hands to snap mo' necks though," Fat Boy said, reaching on the inside of his button up.

Fat Boy pulled out four rolls. He tossed them onto the desk. It all amounted to thirty-two grand.

"Two feet better than one, you dig?" Fat Boy talked in code.

"Yea, I can dig it," Ty stood up from his leather chair.

He pushed the gray file cabinet that sat behind him over, then kneeled and removed two square foot tiles. Tyrone pulled three blocks of cocaine from beneath the floor.

"Now, you retarded nigga, because you got three feet," he joked, placing the drugs onto the desk.

Fat Boy grabbed the blocks of powder from the desk and stuffed them into his red, metal toolbox. There were no tools. He wasn't even an actual employee. He played the part on occasions.

Tyrone replaced the tiles and slid the file cabinet back into it's proper place. He and Fat Boy walked through the office door, entering the auto repair shop.

"What's going on, Mr. Hunter?" a young, dark-complexioned mechanic with a rough stubble of facial hair spoke.

He was replacing a faulty water pump on a silver '02 Nissan Maxima. It was pulled in off of the highway near Quiet Storm's Garage after blowing a tire. Tyrone notified the owner that it was leaking fluids also.

"I'm good. How about yourself, Kyrell?"

"I'm good. The wife is expecting," Kyrell replied nonchalantly.

"Oh shit! Congratulations! That's right on time, 'cause I'm looking to give you that raise you been deserving next month," the boss said proudly.

"I appreciate that, Mr. Hunter," the young mechanic put his head back under the hood of the car.

***

Bandanna Smurf pulled up to Quiet Storm's garage, but not so the silver BMW 350 could be seen in plain view.

"Damn, nigga, the parking lot right there! Why you pull on this side of the curb?" Cherry asked.

"Because ain't going in there. Go get yo' shit!" Smurf demanded to prove his authority in front of Clutch.

"Cuz, hop in the front."

Red Cherry smacked her lips.

"Whatever, nigga. You coming by later on?"

Red Cherry stood outside of the passenger side leaning in.

Commuters were honking their horns at the sexy late-night entertainer who was snug in an all-red body suit.

"I'll call you later," Smurf said, playing half interested.

"Yea, call first, because my daughter might be there."

Red Cherry stood upright and strutted away in her heels. Her curly weave bouncing in the breeze of the Spring.

"I mean dammit, Clutch! That ass is pokin' out! I thank I love that hoe," Smurf studied her stride towards the shop.

"Nigga, remember how she had you fucked up the last time. You need to get focused," Clutch urged his friend as they pulled from the curb.

***

Fat Boy, Kyrell, and a Mexican employee's eyes became fixated on a red ball of fire approaching. Besides Joanne, there wasn't much beauty gracing the shop, just oily mechanics.

Fat Boy immediately began to feel out of his element. The shame of having a 9 to 5 in front of a desirable woman was too much pressure. He reached to adjust the iced-out baby charm around his neck but realized it wasn't there. He'd normally be hopping out of his white Range Rover he had grinded late nights for. But today, he was just a common, greasy auto mechanic.

"What's up, Ty?" Cherry wiggled close by.

She adjusted the short denim jacket to cover her full breast. She saw gawking eyes coming from nothing but unqualified men. If only she hadn't pleasured Tyrone's entourage, maybe, she'd get a shot at a real man in her eyes, Tyrone to be exact.

"We got you up and ready. Your starter needed replacing, but she fires right up now," Ty ushered her towards his office.

Red Cherry came in and sat across from Tyrone's desk. She crossed one hefty thigh over the other.

Tyrone put on his gold frame Cartier glasses before speaking.

"How your daughter Camiya doing?" he asked as he made a copy of the service receipt.

"Oh, she is doing fine. Her and Ta Ta just doing what young girls do best. Being a handful," Cherry said, studying Tyrone at work.

He was casual in a white Lacoste shirt and blue jeans.

"A street nigga that made it and still tapped in. Damn, this nigga too fine! That bitch Joanne lucky. I wanna fuck and suck this nigga off right on this desk with my ass in the air. Marry me, baby. Marry me!"

Tyrone licked his chapped dark lips and caught Red Cherry in a lustful daze. He stood up and locked the latch on the office door. It seemed as if she was irresistible after all. And Tyrone was no stronger than any other man who locked eyes with her.

He stood in front of her wandering eyes, showcasing the print in his tan slacks. Red Cherry was in awe. She couldn't resist brushing her hands across his bulge. It wasn't long before she was gagging as he pushed further into her throat.

Tyrone stripped Red Cherry down out of her red bodysuit. He began sucking on her brown nipples as he pulled her to the edge of the desk. He shoved himself inside of her as she wrapped her legs and heels around his waist.

"I knew that bitch Joanne wasn't fuckin' this nigga right. She couldn't keep you home long enough. But I got you, baby, I got you!" Cherry promised in her thoughts as she leaned her head back and orgasmed.

"Cherry! Cherry!" Tyrone moaned her name repeatedly, coming to a climax.

"Cherry!" He snapped his fingers and interrupted her dream.

"Here you go, Cherry. Ain't hit you too hard. Sixty for the part, thirty-dollar service fee. You my neighbor, plus you keep a close eye on Ta Ta." Ty said and pointed an ink pen for her to grab.

Red Cherry wiped the perspiration from her chest as she rose from the seat to sign the receipt. He removed the pink copy and gave her the yellow form.

"Someone 'll show you to your ride. And I'll see you 'round the way."

Tyrone buzzed his cousin in on the intercom.

"Yea, boss?" Fat Boy showcased his open-faced golds.

"Show this nice lady to her vehicle, please. Thank you," Ty handed Red Cherry her keys.

"This way, Miss," Fat Boy opened the office door, allowing her out first so that he could watch from behind.

"You from 'round here?" he sparked a little dialogue.

"I don't stay too far why?"

"Just hadn't seen you at the shop before," Fat Boy probed.

Red Cherry looked at Fat Boy as they approached her Yukon.

"You look familiar. What's yo' name?"

"Fat Boy," he replied confidently, knowing his reputation proceeded him.

"Fat Boy? Yea, I heard of him. He be in the white Range with the white feet," Red Cherry surmised.

"I be in the white Range, with the white fo's," he baited.

"Nah, not ranging a bell. I might've seen it and paid it no mind."

"I'm 'bout to switch it up soon, though. I just need some new inspiration," he hinted with a bruised ego.

"Like what?" Red Cherry played along. She knew he could be another sponsor for her frivolous wants.

"Like you," he opened the driver's side for her.

"Thank you," she waddled onto the leather of her Chevy SUV.

"Lemme get yo' number 'cause I got so many thangs to do right now. We can get to know each other another time," she dialed Fat Boy into her contacts.

He felt redeemed.

Red Cherry pulled out of the parking lot and hit a left. Two intersections back, Bandanna Smurf and Clutch were driving up on the scene. They pulled into a Bojangles parking lot and waited.

Fat Boy threw his toolbox in the trunk of his beat up '99 Chevy Malibu. He jumped inside, cranked up the bucket, and drove from the scene incognito.

"It's 4:35. I say, he'll be pulling out around 5 o'clock," Smurf estimated.

"That means, I got time to run in here and get a Supreme Dinner with seasoned fries then. You want something?" Clutch said, rubbing his stomach.

"Yea, some chickenwangs, biscuit, seasoned fries, and a iced tea. Oh, and a Bo-Berry biscuit. And make sho' they got seasoning on my fries!"

Chapter 14

Trails

"Hell yea, I'm hungry. That salmon sounds good. Well, look, I'm finishing up. I gotta make a couple runs for some office supplies, then I'll be on the way. Alright. Love you too," Ty ended the call with his fiancée.

Tyrone pulled the CTS-V Cadillac coupe outside of the garage gate. He hopped out and dragged the two metal, chain linked doors over the asphalt until they met. He locked and secured the fence, then turned back to the driver's side.

"Damn. One more thang. I almost forgot," he said, catching himself in error.

He pulled from his Carhart jeans his iPhone and scrolled through the apps. He scrolled until he saw the red icon with a pit bull and pushed it.

Two snarling, red nosed pits were released from an electronic leash. The professionally trained dogs immediately began to case the property for any potential threats.

Bandanna Smurf and Clutch were diving into their Bojangles meals. They almost forgot about what they were there for.

"Shit! There he go," Smurf threw his wings in the box and the box onto the backseat.

"What the fuck taking this nigga so long? He already chained the fence up," Clutch said, observing their prospect, who stood with his phone in hand.

The pursuit of Tyrone was beginning to wear on his patience. Two fierce dogs came running into Clutch's peripheral.

"He must got that new shit, Beware, that just came out. You can release the dogs anytime from your phone," he filled Smurf in on technology 101.

"Man, I don't give no fuck 'bout no Beware! What, you promoting this nigga now? Sounding like a bullshit commercial and shit."

Bandanna Smurf wiped the chicken grease from his mouth and fingers.

"I'ma end up fuckin' yo' bitch ass up," Clutch's eyes bulged, warning Smurf to humble himself.

"Man, fuck that shit you talking 'bout," Smurf retorted.

Tyrone turned his music track list to Mary J's My Life album before jumping onto the busy South Saunders St. Tyrone was eight cars ahead, doing 55 mph. He skipped a few songs before she sang, "Life is only what you make iiiiiiiiiit, when you're feeling down – "

Bandanna Smurf positioned the BMW behind a large Ford Expedition as they trailed in the distance.

"You thank he is going straight to the crib?" Clutch inquired.

"I doubt it. He prolly gotta make a few a runs first," Smurf replied over the Young Jeezy beating out of the speakers.

"Ain't no telling if we be trailing dude through Raleigh all day," Clutch said impatiently.

"We on a full tank," Smurf pointed to the gas meter.

Tyrone answered his phone, "Hey, Grandma! How my favorite lady getting along?"

"I'm doing just fine, suga. Thanking 'bout cooking me some good ol' neckbones, greens, and frying some conebread. I got fo' hardhead churrins I gots to feed, but Granny only got a soft spot for two," the 70-year-old bootleg liquor merchant explained.

Granny wanted her usual. Two ounces of hard and two ounces of powder cocaine. Though she'd called Tyrone hours ago telling him the same thing, she did it again. Senile was her excuse for it.

Tyrone hated dealing in rock unless it was for a select few of people. Even then, it wasn't because he needed to. It was more like a favor that came with a little extra cash on top. The federal guidelines were 18 to 1 for crack, despite it being the same product as the powder cocaine.

Tyrone pulled into Granny's neighborhood slowly, giving the afternoon kids playing, time to vacate the street. He pulled over to the side of the curb and hopped out.

Granny opened the screen door. Wide hips and droopy breasts. The old school image of grandma. Who'd expect Big Momma to be living a savage life.

"Hey baby! Gimme a great big ol' hug. Mmm mmh," she stepped onto the front porch and squeezed Tyrone. The two embraced, rocking from side to side.

"This nigga coming to see grandma and shit. What this old ass bitch want? Go take some meds or somethin'," Smurf spat, then parked near the playground six houses back.

"Hell, if I know. Probably picking up a pie or some shit. Fool, what the fuck wrong with you for real? At least have some respect for your elders," Clutch snapped.

"Nigga, please. Ain't no crooked humanitarian awards coming our way," Smurf replied.

Bandanna Smurf only loved money, sex, and his gang. Old people and children were exempt.

"Nigga, spell humanitarian," Clutch shot back.

"Okay, suga. Drive safe you hear? Granny told Tyrone as he exited the door. She pulled a pre-rolled from under her wig.

"Finna smoke me some reefus, and finish cleaning up my house."

"Granny you off the chain," Ty laughed.

"He out the door already! I guess, grandma ain't make no sweet potato pie fo' her grandbaby," Smurf said cynically.

"That's 'cause he ain't her grandbaby. Grandma is getting off that work. Look, a fiend walking up to her yard now," Clutch used his keen wisdom as he analyzed the scene.

"Ain't that something? Grandma slangin', gettin' to the chicken. It's mo' than just candy and frozen cups. We ought to tie her old ass up," Smurf entertained the thought as he watched the Cadillac in motion.

"Give Ty time to hit the corner," Clutch mentioned as they shifted into gear.

Tyrone was nearing the last stop sign. He turned into a flurry of cars after a brief pause.

"Yea, nigga. I'm on yo' ass Mister Postman!" Smurf joked, pulling into traffic. His comedy more sinister than funny.

Bandanna Smurf was doing the speed limit, seven cars back, trying to remain off of Tyrone's radar. That was the least of their problems. A blue and white Raleigh police cruiser emerged beside them on the right side.

"Stay looking straight ahead, them people on my right," Clutch advised, being careful not to alarm his friend.

Bandanna Smurf tried inching a quick glance.

"Nigga don't look. You know we ain't got no stash spot for these pistols in here."

"Well, what they doing?" Smurf asked, uneasiness in his voice.

"White dick nose mu'fucka keep peeking over here. Won't he just get the fuck on?" Clutch spat through his clinched teeth. He wanted to give off no indication that they were worried.

The uniformed officers suddenly fired the sirens. Blue and white lights began flashing as they took off. Smurf sighed silently.

"Aaagh, yo' heart dropped through yo' ass, didn't it?" Smurf broke the monotony first, acting unphased.

"Nah, bitch, you was scared as shit, trynna convince me," Clutch replied.

Tyrone drove without a care. He was legit. The four ounces of cocaine that Granny preordered were gone. And the seventy-five hundred he had in his middle console could be accounted for. The police stormed past his car without even a glance.

Tyrone turned a right off of Poole Road into his childhood stomping grounds and where he still lived. He drove a couple of short blocks around the corner before pulling over at a long house with a colorful flower bed in the front.

Bandanna Smurf and Clutch went to circle around. They cruised the perimeter and saw a handful of potential drug customers. Tyrone was making his way inside of the house.

"That's the money spot right there. We seen him here before. And like three fiends just went in and out," Clutch observed as they passed the street again.

"Yea, but what's crazy is, Cherry's crib is right on the street behind it. Shit just keep getting better and better. We fin lay on Ty right from the backyard," Smurf gathered his plans.

"Where we going now?" Clutch asked.

"Back to Super 8. Get up with this nigga, Bull. I'ma hit Cherry up later on and see what she got good for me."

"That whip, nigga! Whoop Pissh! That's what," Clutch joked, doing the slave master's whipping motion with his hand.

"Nawl, ain't no whipping me, nigga. You said, get focused, right? I take heed sometimes," Smurf replied seriously.

Chapter 15

Hard Head

Dirty and Sa'von were sitting in the same spot as always, but with more entertainment than just the PlayStation 3 this time.

A red-bone, 18 yr. old girl, a little chubby on the side, a brown-skin 19 yr old with the body of a stripper, and a half black, part Dominican 17 yr. old sat next to Lil Marc, laughing and smoking.

Moon had finally cut off the homemade porno for once in efforts to keep the young ladies from running off. He even hoped that one of the young scrubs would lose their grip, and their female companions would fall weak.

A light tapping rattled the house's backdoor near the kitchen. Moon jumped up from the bar stool. He peeked through the small window curtain. It was a customer, looking to score.

"Where Dirty at? He back there?" the fat lady Phillis asked, waddling through the door's entrance. She resembled Barney in her purple sweatsuit. Crack definitely hadn't affected her weight noticeably.

"Hey, Lil Marc!" she waved, scooting past Moon.

Moon frowned and wrinkled his nose at the thought that had just run through his mind. The next co-star in his amateur porn.

Lil Marc, only thirteen, used to play with her son, tech geek of the neighborhood. But these days, popular mechanics were too immature compared to his thirst for the street life.

"Dirty, what you gon' give me fo' a hundred? Look out fo' me now. I got this old, scary ass cracka down the street with long money," the plus size woman persuaded for a good deal.

Dirty gave her a slab he'd eyeballed without the scale. She gave it a once over and seemed to be satisfied.

The girls paid diligent attention to the exchange of currency between hands. Brown Skin, with a body like a stripper made a mental note to slide next to Dirty in a short moment.

To Dirty's surprise, Barney didn't complain.

"You fixin' to be here fo' awhile?" she asked.

Dirty nodded, then pointed her to the door.

Moon saw a man with a cane approaching in a tan colored Members Only jacket and a matching Kangol. He stepped through the door past the heavy lady making her exit.

"Ol' Moon! You still hanging in there, baby?" he greeted with an unhealthy smile.

In a class of what was once thirty something teeth, he only had seven students in attendance.

"Yea, I'm making it still," Moon replied.

Moon was still in his Nike gear, head to feet as always. He seemed to be doing better than the man that posed the question.

"Where my lil man at?" the customer said, stepping out of the kitchen.

"There he go," he strained once again to smile. Life had burdened even something as simple as his facial expressions.

"Sa'von, what you know good, nephew," he called Young Sanity by his government. He used to deal with his father before he was sent to the feds.

Sa'von hopped off the couch and walked into the kitchen. He really wasn't into having dialogue with men amongst females. Especially the ones he barely knew.

The customer caned his way behind, pulling out three twenty-dollar bills. He gave the old man four large rocks, which could have been broken down for more profit. But Sa'von cut them big because they moved faster, plus, he always got the family price.

The man pulled off his hat and placed the rocks securely inside before placing it back onto his head.

"Boy, you looking just like yo' father," he nudged Sa'von's shoulder.

The young hustler didn't smile at the remark. He hardly ever did.

"And you rarely speak. Just like yo' father," the customer added as he turned away.

"Alright, O.G. Take it easy out there," he told him, watching him exit the door.

Tyrone grabbed the door before it could fully close behind the old man. He stepped inside the kitchen. The disappointment quickly showed. He turned to Sa'von.

"What the fuck do this nigga thank he doing?" Ty spewed, clearly upset.

Tyrone looked at Moon. The old man had nothing to say.

The young lady in a stripper's body had her tongue salivating the side of Dirty's neck. He was smirking, smoking a blunt when Tyrone looked his way.

"Dirty, let me talk to you," Ty said calmly.

Dirty rose nonchalantly as if he was in complete control of everything around him.

"Kaleeya, let me handle something, baby. Keep looking sexy, though," he licked his chapped lips.

Tyrone, Sa'von, Dirty, and Moon stood huddled in the kitchen, inaudible to the girls and Lil Marc.

"How the fuck you 'posed to focus on business with these lil broads in yo' shit? They a distraction. They seen too much already! Tell 'em bye," Ty gave the scolding, then the order.

Dirty tried to keep a cool demeanor in front of company as if he were in control. He felt powerless, but he had to oblige. He headed back towards the living room to convey the parting news to the young ladies.

"Hey, I'ma holla at y'all, Kaleeya."

The leader of the pack looked at Tyrone's movements as he chastised Moon. She got the point.

"Yahtema, Lin, let's go girl," she told her gang.

"It hurt Lil Marc to have to unwrap his arm from around the chubby one's waist. The girls grabbed their small purses and made their exit.

Tyrone looked at Lil Marc still sitting on the couch, puffing weed into the air comfortably.

"You too, lil nigga!"

"I'll get at you, bruh," the 4 ft 8 youngster passed the weed off to Dirty.

"Ain't trying to rain on yo' parade or nothing. But discipline is next to freedom. It's a lot of niggas doing long football numbers behind a female being they downfall," Ty lectured.

Two more customers arrived at the door simultaneously. Their tapping at the door was too loud for comfort.

"Gotdamn, y'all can't knock like you got some sense?" Dirty yelled at the two regulars. Inside, he breathed a sigh of relief they cut Tyrone's lecture short.

"Do something nice fo' me, Quiet Storm, baby," the skinny man with what looked like a worn-out perm, brandished forty dollars.

"I got sixty, Ty. What you gon' do with this one here? He be off the chain out here," the stubby, short one pointed at Dirty.

"Tighten his ass up, Jesse. You know, how y'all raised me. Ain't working though," Ty replied.

"Don't forget what I said, Dirty. I'm 'bout to check on Joanne and hit the shower," he turned to leave.

"I'ma see you, Jesse," he said.

"Be safe cousin," Sa'von exclaimed.

Tyrone stepped outside and saw Tanisha and Camiya walking down the street. He looked at his watch which said 6:30 p.m.

"Ta Ta, you headed to the house for dinner, right?" It was more of a demand than a question.

"Yes. I'm going right now," she confirmed.

"Kids," Ty shook his head, suspecting the girls were up to no good.

Chapter 16

Salty

Wednesday was usually one of the slower days, but this day was an exception. It was one of the busiest Hump Day's that Tyrone had experienced in a year.

The Mexican immigrant, Hector, was shaving the head gaskets on a warped motor of a Mitsubishi Galant. The youngster, Kyrell, was flushing a radiator. And a new recruit, just released on parole, Terrence, was doing a wheel alignment on a Jeep Grand Cherokee.

Tyrone had four trucks out on call and had two more pick up requests. He even had to throw on his uniform to provide his customers with prompt and quality service.

Joanne came in to do the office work, while Tyrone went out with the rest of his wrecker truck drivers. Even Fat Boy stopped by to feed those chaotic pit bulls that only him, Tyrone, and Joanne could get close enough to.

Tyrone was making a run to Capital Boulevard on the north side to pick up two cars from a Spanish community. He was accompanied by another one of his trucks with a qualified driver.

They reached Brentwood East apartments and were signaled over towards the cars by a guy in a cowboy hat and alligator boots with spurs on the back.

Tyrone hadn't noticed, Detective Bob Cornwald and Timmothy Hasselblack sitting in the neighboring parking lot of a convenient store. It was an hour after noon, and they were still eating doughnuts and drinking coffee.

"Look at this coonbuggy, thanking he can change his suit and not be a po'ch monkey. He acts as if he's the street's Messiah, providing jobs to ex-cons, masquerading as a common blue-collar citizen," Hasselblack spewed his train of thought from behind the wheel.

Both detectives were only in their late forties, but their ideologies could be attributed to a long lineage of hereditary hate. Though they were easy on the eyes, their relationships with women were in constant ruins due to their racist views.

"I'll bet you any amount of money, Cornwald, that them boys are transporting cocaine in them-there vehicles. I say they're right in the trunk," Hasselblack wagered.

"I got a crispy hundred-dollar bill on it," Cornwald accepted.

"Awl, I ain't a gamblin' man, Cornwald. I was just saying that this boy, Tyrone Coon Hunter, is making moves right up under our pearl noses. Do you remember the boy that Homicide Unit found dead in the chicken coop? What a cowinky-dink he got his oil checked two days outta the week at his garage. Now, he's dead. Lethal injection. Subtle. Just his style. And who gets their oil changed that frequent?"

"Okay, let's say you're right, Hassel. We don't have a probable cause. And we wouldn't be able to get the judge to sign off on a warrant quick enough for this route. He'll be history and back on the south by then," Cornwald surmised.

Disgusted, Hasselblack shook his head from side to side.

"Hell, you wanna do things by the book? You can do 9-1-1 response. But this here's Detective Unit! And I detect that there's drugs in them cars they're about to haul!" Hasselblack furiously pointed at the wreckers.

"You back up and chain the Lincoln Town Car, DeSean. I'll take the Mercury," Ty said as he felt the sudden urgency to relieve himself."

"You mind if I use your baño, Mr. Gomez?"

"Si, no problemo, vato. Vamonos," Gomez said as Tyrone followed.

DeSean hopped from the wrecker and began loading the Lincoln in normal wrecker fashion. Tyrone came back moments later and mounted the Mercury. They both turned on the trucks emergency lights as required by the NCHP Wrecker Service Regulations.

"You see, Cornwald, just look at those rollbacks. They're top of the line, late models, unconventional, even rotating carriers!" Hasselblack pointed out the perks from the driver's seat of the Crown Victoria.

"You sure do know a helluva lot about trucking, Hassel. Was that your dream or something?" Cornwald quizzed, biting down on a glazed strawberry jelly from Krispy Kremes.

"Na'an, it was a dream of my old man's. Never could afford to follow up on it with his cop's salary. But this punk, Hunter here, is parading around, like he got Quiet Storm's Tow and Recovery legitimately!" Hasselblack said. Envious and racially motivated, he shifted into gear.

Two more interections until Tyrone reached his shop alongside DeSean. He'd noticed what looked like an undercover car trailing him for the last fifteen minutes. Undeterred, he pulled the truck and its tow past the gates.

The tow boss stepped from his wrecker, while the detectives wasted no time in opening their doors and emerging in plain sight.

"Welcome to Quiet Storm's, officers. Where our customers are served quality deserved!" Ty initiated, offering a pretentious smile.

"Yea, I bet," Hasselblack said sarcastically, though Tyrone heard it and disregarded the taunt.

"Will you be needing any of our customary services?" Ty asked nicely. By now, DeSean had parked the truck and came over to Tyrone's side in concern.

Hassleblack went straight in for the kill.

"Were you aware that these cars you pulled from Brentwood East were used to transport stolen goods?" he questioned.

"Stolen goods, huh? That's the best he could come with?" Ty figured subconsciously.

"No, sir, I wasn't aware of their past. But as of today, I have not the slightest doubt that these cars are sanitary.

So, how could I be of any assistance for that matter?" he quizzed.

Joanne saw the scene from the office monitor, then came walking out with her iPhone recording the standoff. Tyrone's mechanics were working half-heartedly, giving their attention to the parking lot.

"What the hell is that she's holding?" Hasselblack inquired of the new Apple device.

"Well, you can start by opening the trunk of those two cars you just brought in," Cornwald suggested in a commanding tone.

"I don't think I can do that without a warrant, detective," Ty declined the offer.

Joanne had the camera of the smartphone focused still.

"Now, is it anything else I can do for you? A tune up, a oil change, windshield wiper fluid perhaps? It's on the house."

The two detectives turned their attention towards the smartphone recording their every move. They had to come with something better next time.

"You people have a nice day. We'll be seeing you around, Storm," Hasselblack winked his right eye before hopping back in the driver's seat.

Tyrone turned and walked towards his building's entrance.

"The way the cop said my name you'd swear he know me. Can't he see it say Ty on my shirt?" he said, tugging at his uniform.

The couple stepped inside the office and Tyrone sat down agitatedly in his desk chair.

"I don't know, baby. Maybe, it's just him fishing and nothing else. But you can believe that they will go back and do they little homework before they come at you again. So, just be careful."

"Yea, with fake testimonies from niggas ain't never seen. I seen this game before. But I got big plans fo' me. They gotta come a lil harder!"

"Plans for you? That's it?" Joanne meditated on the statement for a moment.

It felt like little straight pins sticking through her heart. Her mind processed that she wasn't a part of her so-called future husband's plans. But luckily, she had a plan of her own.

If Tyrone left her today, she'd be back at square one. Anytime after her plan took effect, would be different, though. She vowed that she would be compensated for the time she put in. And no man would leave her high and dry again.

Chapter 17
Missfits

Camiya and Tanisha were on the sofa, watching The Boondocks cartoon series. Red Cherry wasn't home as usual, giving the two young girls more freedom and the opportunity to make their own mistakes.

The living room was foggy from the weed that Tanisha supplied for her and her friend. They both were giggling, tipsy off of the opened bottle of Alize, Camiya found in her mother's bedroom.

"Girl, I'm bored. I damn near know every episode of The Boondocks line for line. Won't you call Lil Marc over here?" Tanisha suggested receiving a crazed look from her friend.

"Shit, you know, Lil Marc ain't coming over here, not inside this house!" Camiya retorted.

"Why he won't?" Tanisha inquired unconvinced.

"Because, you know that he knows that, Dirty knows, that yo' ass is over here!" Camiya said, waving the Red Passion bottle in the air.

"Girl, damn all that, you know, and he know, and she know, sounding like a Shawty Lo."

The two shared a brief laugh.

"What's all that supposed to mean?" Tanisha said bluntly.

"Ta, Lil Marc is scared of Dirty. He ain't nothing but thirteen. And what's yo' cousin, like eighteen? He be out here messing with guns and beating people ass up and down the street. That boy ain't crazy," Camiya stopped talking and crossed her legs.

The young and immature Camiya swore she had everything in life down to a science. The you-can't tell-her-nothing-she-don't already-know type.

"Well, how about, he come and Dirty come too?" Tanisha shifted the balance of power in her direction.

Camiya suddenly became thirsty. And it wasn't for more Alize.

"Dirty, come down here too!" she adjusted her clothes.

Camiya checked for wrinkles in her pink shirt and flaws in her skirt. Then, she jumped up to go to rub some lotion on her ankles. Tanisha had to wipe away her tears from laughter.

When Camiya walked back into the front room, she had an entirely different fit on. Her skirt was tighter than the one she previously had on.

"Look at yo' fast ass, being grown," Tanisha scrutinized her friend's actions.

"Compared to you, I am grown. And fourteen makes me growner than you," she replied.

"Whatever. So, did you call him?"

"Yea, I called Lil Marc's phone. He says he coming and my baby coming too," Camiya blushed.

"What you say?"

"I asked, did he have some weed to sell. Hold up, you asking me all these questions. Is yo' momma still at work, Ta Ta?" Camiya inquired.

"Yea, her and my daddy. They probably be back around time 106 and Park halfway through. They say it's been really busy today, since you know, spring break coming up 'n' all," Tanisha replied.

"Oh, okay. I had to ask, 'cause you know how they is."

A light knock was heard tapping on the front door. The two young girls grew optimistic. Camiya looked through the peephole. She blew her breath into her palms and failed the stink test.

"Needs candy," she scurried to the candy bowl on the coffee table, then back to the door.

Dirty stepped in, then Lil Marc followed. He shared a resemblance to the rapper-actor Bow Wow. They shared the same low-cut Caesar, similar eyes and the same complexion.

"What the fuck y'all doing? Ain't shit conducive, like schoolwork going on in here," Dirty interrogated the girls.

"Boy, please, you probably ain't never did a lick of homework in yo' life. And I doubt you even know how to spell conducive or know what it means," Camiya spat.

Dirty waved off the challenge. He didn't know how to spell it.

"Psssh, lil girl," he dismissed.

"Anyway, you got the bud, Lil Marc?" she changed the subject.

"Yea, I got it," Lil Marc said in his underdeveloped voice.

Lil Marc pulled out a bag weighing 3.5 grams of some mild colored mid-grade.

Camiya pulled out some cash from her tight skirt pocket.

Lil Marc grabbed the money and headed for the door.

"Hold on, nigga, damn! Why you so in the rush? Y'all ain't gon' smoke with me and your cousin, Dirty?" Camiya asked, trying not to be so obvious.

Dirty turned and looked at Tanisha. She tried to look as naïve as possible.

"What the hell these lil mu'fuckas up to?" he asked himself quietly.

"Yea. Let's smoke. Fuck it," he said.

Camiya stood up from the couch and left a spot for Lil Marc to six next to Tanisha. She moved to the loveseat instead.

Dirty had no choice but to sit next to her after Lil Marc took his seat. He pulled a cigar from his ear as Camiya began rolling her weed.

"Where the hell yo' momma at, girl?" Dirty looked at Camiya suspiciously.

Shoulder length hair. A face and skin like her mother's; she was well on her way, he observed.

"Oh, she with her friend, Alexus," she answered.

Dirty's mind commenced to clicking instantly.

"Miss Cherry thicker than a Snicker. But shit, I'll tear lil Camiya's red ass up she keeps fuckin' round!" he studied as her lips continued to move.

"Yo' shoes cu... you stay fresh, sh... buy m... so... this weekend. You... a girlfriend? Is you even listening to me?" Camiya stopped rambling.

"Yea, I'm listening," he lied.

Dirty was too busy noticing how her hips were spreading out more lately. Everything she was saying sounded distorted at the moment.

"So, you gon' do that?" Camiya asked once more to confirm things.

"I got you," Dirty unknowingly agreed to buying her the same identical Jordans on his feet.

Dirty turned and looked Tanisha and Lil Marc curiously.

"What the fuck they thank they 'posed to have going on over there?"

Lil Marc sat, sweating in his palms, trying to spark conversation.

"What you got on your mind, Ta?" he asked timidly.

"Nothing, just wondering why you don't be speaking when you with, Dirty?" Tanisha responded.

"Dirty be acting up sometimes. He just be playing though about us not talking. He don't be serious."

Tanisha felt relieved.

Twenty minutes and another Boondock's episode later, the living room was full of bloodshot eyes. All of a sudden, Dirty hopped up from the couch and grabbed Camiya's hand. They carried the remainder of the weed with them.

"Oh, shit!" Tanisha whispered into Lil Marc's ear, watching the two disappear into Red Cherry's bedroom.

Dirty had no concern for what Tanisha was doing any longer. The only thing he was worried about was taking advantage of her young friend, Camiya. Never mind the statutory rape guidelines that could be presented in a Wake County courtroom.

"What they up to?" Lil Marc quizzed.

"What you thank?" Tanisha shot cynically in her country accent.

"So, what you trynna do? It look like Dirty too busy to be worried with us," Tanisha gazed into Lil Marc's brown eyes.

Lil Marc made his move. He leaned in and kissed Tanisha. He eased her back into a lateral position on the couch. Abruptly, she pushed him off.

"We need to go in Camiya's room," she advised.

Lil Marc grew ecstatic, but nervous at the same time.

Barely in their teens, Lil Marc and Tanisha lie deep into one another on the bed. They were both young, but Marc couldn't help but wonder in the midst of passion, why he seemed to be the nervous one. He intended to be more delicate with Tanisha than he'd been with the chubby, red-bone, Yahtema, he'd last had sex with.

Chapter 18

Farfetched

Joanne came through the door in her home and kicked off her heels immediately. It wasn't that the office work exerted a lot of energy, it was a case of her rarely having to lift a finger that had her exhausted.

Tyrone followed in, unbuttoning his work uniform. He kicked his soiled construction Timberlands off at the door and secured the locks.

"Baby don't worry about cooking. Just call Pizza Express. Order beef pepperoni for the night. I know neither one of us is in the mood," Ty suggested with a distant look on his face.

"What's wrong Ty? That situation at work still on your mind?" Joanne quizzed.

They never discussed in full detail the undercovers trailing him through Raleigh. Tyrone only spoke freely in what he considered safe zones free of devices.

"I wonder how long they been trying to build a case."

Tyrone paced the floor repeatedly. He was creating a path in the plush money green carpet.

"I'm about to fall back, though," Ty said, finally giving the carpet a rest.

He sat next to Joanne on the couch.

"So, what you gonna do? Besides today, the business has been a little slow," Joanne said concerningly.

"I'm just gonna take a leap of faith with what I got. I'm 'bout ready to make this expansion. I got to run down to Atlanta tomorrow and get with this property owner. He got a couple of empty garages I need to look at. Business gonna be three times what it is here," Ty foreshadowed.

Joanne's face took on a disgruntled expression. She wasn't happy. Tyrone could just up and leave anytime he felt, while she felt trapped and confined to his world and his dreams.

Her body and natural beauty had taken her a long way from her troubled past. She came from Detroit's east and west side to the trenches in East Durham at Buttafly's home. Now, with the finances she needed in arm's reach, it was time to break free and pursue her own dreams.

"I see you sitting over there, looking like that. I promise, after I get my shops right, me and you gonna travel the world. I don't mean just South Beach in Miami either. I'm talking crystal clear waters of Bimini in the Bahamas!" he promised as he eased up from the couch.

Tyrone kneeled down at his woman's feet and palmed one of them in his hands. He began to massage her foot as she relaxed her body and began to disperse the built-up tension.

The way that Tyrone was using his hands turned Joanne on to the max. She leaned her head back onto the couch as her panties became soaked from her juices.

Suddenly, Tyrone caught a glimpse of the time from the G-Shock on his wrist. His militant side kicked in.

"It's 6:30, call Ta Ta and tell her come 'cross the street," he stood up and headed for the bedroom.

Joanne was more aggravated now that Tyrone had started something without finishing. She pulled out her phone. How to Love by Lil Wayne played for about 15 seconds before her daughter answered.

"Little girl, I know damn well you seen we had come home. Bring your ass!" she yelled before hanging up.

Tanisha stuck her key in, then untwisted the locks. Her agitated mother stepped from the kitchen as she tried to make a swift retreat to her room.

"What took you so long? And did you do your homework?" Joanne interrogated.

"Yea, I did it," Tanisha said, dropping her backpack.

"Okay. Well, I want to see it after we eat."

"What we eating?"

"I ordered from Pizza Express. Anyway, Ty is going to Atlanta tomorrow. I'ma be working until five on Thursday and Friday. So, you need to make sure to do what I ask concerning this house and your schoolwork," Joanne commanded.

Tanisha sat down beside her mother, and she grabbed the remote. She flipped the Time-Warner Cable channel to 106 & Park.

"Child, y'all gonna run yourself crazy behind this 106 & Park. You know I got that Soulja Boy dance down now. Ty, he don't know how to have no fun," Joanne sighed.

"What Camiya been up to lately?" she asked, glancing at her daughter's foggy eyes.

Tanisha did 98 percent of what she was supposed to as a child and a student. She brought home A's and B's. Her priorities seemed to be in order. In return, Joanne untightened the leash a bit.

"Oh, Camiya? She alright."

"What about Cherry crazy ass? I hear she got a new friend now."

"Some man been coming over lately. He always wearing the same clothes all the time. He funny lookin', kind of short. I was leaving anyway because she had just came in with her friends," Tanisha said, concentrating on the Chris Brown video.

A knock on the door breached the mother-daughter convo. Joanne stood up and looked through the peephole.

"Hey Miss Jo Jo!" Camiya said once the door swung open.

"Come on in, Camiya," Joanne stepped aside.

"My momma trippin'. Can I sit here for a little while?"

Joanne gestured towards the couch.

"Look, Ta, when the pizza man come, hand him this. Don't open the door for nobody else," Joanne said counting out twenty-five dollars and then a tip.

Joanne left the living room. She walked into the bedroom and saw Tyrone packing a few personal belongings.

"I gave Tanisha the money to pay the pizza man. Her and Camiya in the front," she said, placing her hands on her curvy hips.

"You gon' love me long time tonight before you leave?" she enticed with the batting of her eyelashes.

Tyrone looked up at his astonishing fiancée. Her round backside stuffed in the indigo stretch denim caused him to rock up in his boxers.

"Baby, come on now. What kind of question is that? You know I gotta eat up all that 'fore I go," he grinned.

Joanne sat on the king-sized bed, watching Tyrone gather several small items. She was vigilant as he stepped into the closet as she hoped he would.

Tyrone kneeled down to the level of his secluded safe. He exposed the wall, then turned the dial to the right on the first combination number. He felt Joanne's body heat after scrolling left to the second.

"Oh, I see. You want some Kinky Kells in the closet shit, huh?"

Tyrone stopped scrolling.

"Damn, I almost got the third number!" Joanne thought, disappointed.

"I'm thirsty for daddy's dick in my mouth. Let's get in the shower!" she immediately said as a decoy.

"I'll wait until she sleeping to open this shit up. Her ass been acting strange lately. Must think I'm hiding some rubbers in the safe," Ty pondered the thought.

"Okay, let's get it," he said aloud and laughed it off.

Chapter 19

Young Pain

At Ligon Middle School, Tanisha and Camiya both sat in I.S.S. for continuously interrupting their 8th grade science class. Although Miss Taylor enjoyed the two's comradery, she would not have it at the expense of the other students trying to focus. She sat back watching her In-School-Suspension troublemakers like a trained rottweiler.

"Girl, would you look at what Miss Taylor got on," Camiya texted with a laughing emoji.

"Smh. Lol. What the fuck Geno keep peeking back here for? Is he coming to the party Friday night?" Tanisha texted Camiya.

"Yea, I think so. But I hope yo cousin Dirty and that nigga Sa'von don't show. You know they beat him and his homeboy up," Camiya texted.

The school bell rang, signaling the end of the day as Tanisha was about to send another text. The friends hastily stuffed their papers into their handbags and sprinted for the door as if they were escaping a dungeon and Miss Taylor, was the dragon.

"Hold on, Miss Tanisha Hill. I just received information from the head office that a guardian is here to pick you up. He said, he's driving his silver Cadillac today."

"Oh, okay. Thank you! See you Miss Taylor," Tanisha said, then scurried out the door.

Camiya looked at Tanisha suspiciously as they made their way through the crowded hallway of students.

"Girl, that's Dirty I bet, playing games as always. He must've got somebody to rent out they car," Tanisha responded to her friend's inquiring mind.

Lil Marc was coming out of his classroom when he spotted the two girls from his neighborhood speeding by. He took a look at Tanisha in her jean skirt and neon pink leggings, then sped into high gear.

"Damn, slow y'all asses down! Who out there so important got y'all running all crazy?" Lil Marc said, not liking the fact that his crush wasn't racing towards him.

"We trynna see who out here that's 'posed to be picking her up in a silver Lac," Camiya said while devoting her attention straight ahead.

"I bet y'all actin' thirsty for no reason. That's probably Dirty," Lil Marc guessed as they all pushed past the school's double doors.

Through the cluster of different students finding their assigned yellow buses, Camiya spotted the car first.

The silver Cadillac DTS Deville sitting on vogue tires, reflected the bright and cloudy day off its factory chrome rims. The host was riding clean, but past the 15 percent mirror tint, Tanisha couldn't get a clear view of the occupant.

111

The horn honked twice. A hand emerged from the driver-side window with two gold rings signaling Tanisha over. Camiya tagged along beside her friend while Lil Marc waited alert in the distance. The window slid back up.

Tanisha walked around towards the passenger side. When the window came down, her face took on an apparent expression of uneasiness.

Tanisha tucked her bag in her right arm and made a U-turn back towards her friend.

"Who is that?" Camiya quizzed, puzzled by the swift reaction.

Not seeing any signs of happiness, the driver stepped out of the car with a white stick hanging from his lips. In his dark green Mauri gators, colorful shirt and black slacks, he approached the young girls.

"Long time no see, princess," he said as he removed the grape lollipop from his mouth.

"My name is Buttafly, lil lady," he looked at Camiya, demanding her attention.

"Ta Ta's father," he added.

"Come on, Miya. Let's get on the bus," Tanisha said, then rudely turned. Halfway through, her right arm was grabbed.

Lil Marc was no longer observing. He began moving in towards Tanisha and the unfamiliar man standing in her personal space. Buttafly released her arm at the sight of the young scrapper in black jeans and a red Chicago Bulls hat tilted up.

"Tanisha, you good?" he asked aggressively.

Buttafly smirked and even held back a laugh.

"Yea, she's good Lil Bow Wow. She 'bout to ride in style, like she supposed to," he replied.

Buttafly looked back at Tanisha and stuck the grape flavored sucker onto his tongue again.

"Nah, I know 'er too good to know she ain't straight," Lil Marc barked back.

"You young niggas way too feisty these days. Home is on the decline because the recession hurt the Asiatic Black man the most. Got you in a rush to die fast and get to hell quick," Buttafly said in a voice as smooth as Keith Sweat's.

"Asiatic? Who the fuck is this Fruity Pebbles lookin' ass nigga thank he talking to?" Lil Marc said heatedly from the blatant disrespect.

"Look, Ta Ta, just hop in the car before I have to fuck-"

"Befo' you have to what? Yeen about to do shit," Lil Marc went under his black and red Polo shirt. He pulled a black 25 automatic from underneath his shirt.

Once again, Buttafly chuckled out loud at the sight.

"Exactly, what I was saying. The plight of the black demographic. I'ma go and get out yo' way, young scrap 'fore you be done shot one of these kids. You know you young niggas can't shoot. See you, Princess," Buttafly backstepped.

"Nah, I swear I won't miss," Lil Marc held the gun low to keep from making a scene.

Buttafly hopped back into the leather seat of the Cadillac and turned up the volume on his Purple Rain cd. He eased from the curb slowly and cruised away as if he owned the road.

"Hurry up and put that gun away," Camiya said as Lil Marc obliged. She turned and looked at Tanisha.

"Shit, I thought, Tyrone Hunter was yo' daddy. The way you was acting with him that just left, I would've never guessed."

"After the way he treated my momma, and the shit he did to me, I should've let Lil Marc shoot his ass," Tanisha replied with an unexpected answer.

Lil Marc didn't know what to say. He just looked confused. All he knew was, he had protected Tanisha even at the expense of him getting permanently expelled from school. And if that was her father, it was a strong possibility she'd have to deal with him again soon.

"What did he do to you, Ta Ta? If he hurt you, you know me and Dirty 'll.... "

Tanisha abruptly broke into the middle of Lil Marc's premeditated death plot.

"There go a Universal Cab pulling up! We catching that. Hey, fo' five!" she yelled out the cab number, waving him over.

The African immigrant had the best sound system over any cab in the city. And on the outside, he was sitting on 24-inch rims that looked like chrome dinner plates. At Tanisha's request, he blasted Mook Dig's latest rap cd.

Tanisha had avoided answering Lil Marc's questions, but he had his own theory in mind. Her flower wasn't so delicate for one reason, and he believed it was because of an ugly Buttafly.

Chapter 20

Headlights

Getting up two hours earlier on Friday for work had paid off for Joanne. She spent nearly an hour just perfecting her make-up.

Her gold eye shadow was light, but luminating at the same time. Her cheek bones were defined and bold from primping them to her desired likeness. And her lips were immaculate with a hint of shimmering lip gloss.

Joanne sat at the boss' desk in her boss uniform. A knee-length tan skirt covered her bottom half. And a matching, thin button-down collar covered her top.

Her long, black hair was pulled back into a tight ponytail. She was beautifully clad but was careful not to excite Tyrone's male employees by parading in their faces.

The Spring weather of March had a lot to do with the garage's continuous activity. The wrecker trucks were bringing in cars and SUVs back-to-back. Even an older model tow truck was brought into Quiet Storm's Tow and Recovery garage.

The auto mechanics were busy with installments and repairs. And Joanne had chipped a manicured nail while typing in business operations data.

The office phone rang, and she picked up on line 1.

"Quiet Storm's Tow and Recovery! Joanne speaking!"

"Hey, Ho'anne," an elderly woman spoke.

"It's Jo-Anne, ma'am," she corrected.

"Oh, ah hoo hoo! Pardon me, sweetie."

"It's no problem. Now, what can I do for you?"

"Y'all do wish-uh-wipuhs?"

"Do we wish for wipers? I'm sorry, I don't understand what you mean, ma'am," Joanne said cordially.

"Wish-uh-wipe-uh," the elderly lady repeated.

"Um, I'm still not clear on what you're saying. Can you speak a little clearer?"

"Wish-uh-wipuh, wish-uh-wipuh, wish-shield-wiperrrr! Dumb bitch! Can you understand that?" The dial tone greeted Joanne.

"Fuck you, you old hag! I guess that's what happens when ain't no young dick in your life. That's why I keep me some on standby," the boss lady laughed, hanging up the receiver.

Joanne pushed the intercom to transmit her voice to the repair shop.

"Hector, did the dogs get fed?"

The Mexico City native tapped on the glass door before being told to enter. He couldn't see past the full-length blinds that were closed shut.

"Si, Senor Gordo Muchacho eleven."

"Gracias, Hector. Buen trabajo," Joanne tested out her Spanish before Hector made his exit.

"I think I said good job."

Joanne looked at the digital numbers on the desk's clock. It read 12:05. She was starving.

"Where the hell is this fool with my lunch," she complained.

"Mane, I'm telling you. You need to get on board. It be so many women coming up here to get simple thangs done. Antifreeze and brake fluids filled; a damn interior light bulb replaced. You know they can't have no mane doing shit like that," Kyrell advised while securing a red Honda's car battery.

"The one that dropped this Accord off bad as hell, bruh! Thick chocolate thang. She 'bout twenty fo'."

"Then why the fuck you ain't get at 'er then? Ain't fixing no damn cars nigga. I got better shit to do. That's yo' job," Dirty said, holding the warm Chinese food from Wangs Kitchen in hand.

Kyrell held up his left hand. He stuck out his ring finger.

"So," Dirty said, shrugging his shoulders.

"Fuck that 'posed to mean?"

"I'ma married mane. I gotta stay out of trouble," Kyrell said halfheartedly. His twenties were over in his mind.

"Sucker-fo'-love-ass-nigga. My aunt food getting cold, listening to yo' loc ass," Dirty said, dismissing the young and faithful.

Dirty headed for the office laughing to himself. He tapped on the glass of the wood door.

"Come in," Joanne yelled.

"Nigga, what took you so damn long?"

"Fuckin' with one of yo' clown ass workers, talking about me getting on the schedule."

"Sit the food on the microwave. Come to think, it wouldn't be such a bad idea!"

"Why's that? Oh, never mind me. I see," Dirty said.

Joanne slid the rolling chair out from behind the wood desk. She planted her Coach heels onto the floor and parted her thighs.

"Yea, you was hungry alright," Dirty said cynically.

"Boy, shut up and come over here," the boss lady commanded.

Joanne lifted her skirt. She had no panties on, showcasing her shaved lower lips.

"I cleared the road so you can navigate better when you suck this pussy," she said as she used her middle finger to stroke herself.

Dirty kneeled to the floor in front of her. He placed his palms under her bottom, then rolled her body closer to his face.

Joanne's eyes were rolling into the back of her head. She had no idea that the first time he went down on her would feel so good. After orgasming on his tongue, she wanted to return the favor.

"You can play the boss, baby!" she advised.

Joanne stood up from the leather chair, leaving it wet with a trail of her juices.

Dirty sat down and unzipped his Polo jeans. His head popped out like a Jack-in-a-box. She took it into the threshold of her throat. Her tongue was on his balls as he pushed fully inside of her mouth.

Crystal tapped Kyrell on the shoulder as he tightened the clips onto a radiator hose. He nearly hit his head on the hood of the car from being startled.

"Hey! What's up, Crystal?" he greeted her.

"Joanne back there?"

"Yea. Twan just brought her lunch."

"Brought her lunch, huh. Oh, okay. Thank you," Crystal said, marching off.

Kyrell put his head back up under the hood. He had no idea what he'd just done.

Crystal approached the door, seeing the blinds were closed as they usually were. She turned the handle down. It opened.

It was the same bare behind Crystal would have to wipe when he was a kid. Dirty's eyes were closed while he was being swallowed whole. He was kicking his feet as if he was eating ice cream.

"Y'all two stupid muthafuckas ain't even got sense enough to lock the door!" Crystal exclaimed with her arms folded.

Joanne jumped up and adjusted her skirt. Dirty put his business back into his pants as Joanne rushed to shut the office door.

"Don't worry, I won't make a scene. I was in the area so, I thought I'd let you know that your mother-in-law, and your grandmother, Antwan Clee – " Crystal paused and looked at her nephew in disgust.

"Is in the hospital at Wake Med right now as you sit here fucking this bitch!"

Crystal walked towards the office door, then turned around. She knew then that she had the leverage she needed over Joanne.

"I couldn't get in touch with Ty, and I see why, Dirty here, couldn't be reached either. But I'll be on my way. Now, y'all get back y'all fun."

Crystal walked out smoothly as if she were of no disturbance. Joanne watched the door close shut, lost for words to describe what just happened. She looked at Dirty with fire in her eyes.

And as for Antwan "Dirty" Hunter; he instantly felt guilty for the betrayal of Tyrone. Nor was not being there for the woman who raised him settling well in his stomach.

Chapter 21

Sight's Set

"I am telling you, youngblood. You needs to go to Wake Med on New Bern and see yo' granny," Moon suggested while cracking a can of Miller High Life.

"Man, O.G., I can't see her like that. That's my momma for real. The lady that took off to Houston and left me with my pops Clee, just birthed me. But that's my momma at Wake Med," Dirty emphasized, masking his yearning for his biological mother.

"Let me tell you something, youngblood. I ain't never had no churrins and that's my regrets. Hopefully, I wouldn't have been a fiend fo' a father, but that's besides the point. It'll eat you all the way to the grave not knowing what she wanted to say to you," Moon said, then gulped his beer as if it were pain medicine.

"Honestly, I already got enough regrets to last a lifetime and straight to the casket," Dirty replied, standing up from the couch.

He made his way towards the kitchen door.

"Be back. I'm finna hit the stash so you can whip up."

Dirty entered the backyard which was fenced in by a wooden gate that had a few missing boards. He treaded towards a rusty toolshed.

***

Clutch sat at the table in the kitchen of Red Cherry's home. He adjusted the binoculars to peer through the vacant spaces in Moon's wooden fence. He watched Dirty pull a blunt from his jeans, look around, then spark the tail-end of it.

Dirty blew out the thick haze of smoke as he observed a black bird revel in the blue afternoon sky scattered with clouds. He glared at the soaring wings for a moment, then decided on a prayer.

"What the fuck is this lil nigga doing – praying?" Clutch wondered what was going on with his mark.

"Dear, God. Why I gotta be so young, going through this much pain? I know you seen me out here slangin'. I done bust a few niggas that was in the way. And I know I done fucked… damn, 'xcuse me, messed up when I laid down with my uncle's fiancée. But I'm ready fo' you to take it out on me. Don't punish momma. She been too good. If you keep her safe, I promise to start over with a clean slate. That's if you let me. That's it God. I'm done."

Dirty rolled a tool cabinet from the middle of the shed's floor, careful not to ruin his Bred 11 Jordans. He had no idea that God wasn't the only one watching over him from afar.

"Come up outta there lil nigga. I got a feeling you got something I need." Clutch watched diligently.

Dirty pulled a white and black striped bag out from underneath a hole in the floor, then pushed the metal cabinet back to its original place. He dusted off his Polo jeans and headed for the gate's entrance. Clutch's eyes followed until he was out of sight, past Moon's kitchen door.

"Clutch, I see you got a scope on they ass." Blue Bull said, stepping into the kitchen, smoking a joint.

Blue Bull was still trying to readjust from smoking out of toilet paper wraps during his 7-year prison bid.

"Yea, I been had the scope on fool while you was shackin' up with blondie from the club. We started to thank yo' ass sanked in the pussy. Thought I was gon' have to run up in there myself to find you. She is finer than a mu'fucka. I woulda did it with the quickness too," Clutch laughed cynically.

"Yea, picture that. Please. Me getting' drowned in some pussy. I see you got jokes. Pipe down and hit the weed, nigga."

Blue Bull reached with the joint.

"Institutionalized ass nigga," Clutch told him.

***

"Tomorrow," Dirty said, sitting the bag on the counter.

"Tomorrow what, nephew?" Moon quizzed.

"I'll go see, Ma, tomorrow."

"There might not be a tomorrow, youngster," Moon said without all the sugarcoating.

"That's just when I'll be ready, O.G." Dirty replied.

Clutch put the binoculars down onto the table.

"Twelve o'clock. That's when we do this. We gone show the homie a Bull City night out."

"These niggas slow. They wouldn't see a Amtrak coming at 'em," Blue Bull added his stamp.

"Smurf still in there fuckin'?" Clutch asked.

"Yea, I could hear that nigga from the living room. He made me wanna kick the door down with my dick in my hand. That pussy must be amazing!" Blue Bull guessed by the noises he could hear.

Red Cherry was using her throat like a vacuum to extract Bandanna Smurf's last drop of semen. She was sure to have him at her beck and call with her award worthy head game.

"Damn, Cherry! I ain't never had my dick sucked like that befo'. Baby, I love you!" Smurf spoke, thinking with his lower head.

Red Cherry wiped the remaining nut from the corners of her mouth before speaking.

"Well, if you love me, nigga, you'd make sure this rent is paid tomorrow. Because ain't got it," she said with her best poker face.

Bandanna Smurf felt a sense of pride to be laying next to a woman as fine and as voluptuous as Red Cherry. Tanisha was right. He was funny looking. But most preferred the term, ugly. He was short on the money, but after tonight, he felt he'd have enough to bargain with.

"I got you, baby. You don't need to worry about shit as long as you giving me this type of lovin'. And plus, I like this neighborhood. I'm thanking 'bout sticking around town a lil bit and doing some damage," Smurf lightly chuckled.

His laugh was cynical, but Red Cherry had no idea that her neck of the woods was in for a rude awakening.

Chapter 22

Breathe Easy

Joanne stood on her front porch amid the dark evening, smoking a cigarette. Her mind was a nervous wreck, contemplating how she could clean up the mess she had spilled in her life. Luckily, her daughter was away at Camiya's aunt's house to attend a party. The distress she was in would've easily been detected by Tanisha.

"How could I have been so damn stupid to leave the door unlocked? I got caught with my future husband's nephew's dick in my mouth. Now, how the hell that look?" Joanne asked herself while her fingers twitched as she took long drags from the Newport.

"I got to think about me and my daughter's future now. The marriage 'll be off for damn sure. I ain't got no money. No job. Nowhere to stay. No family here."

A tear out of desperation ran down Joanne's cheek. Time was ticking, and she hadn't a minute to waste. Unfortunately for her, she hadn't the slightest plan.

***

Crystal stood in Moon's driveway, waiting for her nephew to come out of the door. Her arms were folded as her foot tapped the concrete displaying her impatience.

Dirty stepped out with a black Miami Heat fitted tipped low, barely showcasing his eyes. Underneath the brim of his hat, he looked at his aunt distastefully.

"Fuck you looking at me like that fo', Twan?" she asked.

"Because I know you want something."

"Yea. Nigga, you right. I got fifteen dollars."

Dirty sucked his teeth and sighed angrily. He was getting aggravated at the fact of his father's sister coming to him for favors.

"You stay trynna run game, Cryssy. And you supposed to had quit anyway. I can't keep on serving you shit. Moon gonna catch on if you keep coming over here. He let Ty know everythang that's going on."

"Nigga, fuck what somebody else got to say! You is grown." Crystal pointed at Dirty's chest.

"And I say you been grown since like twelve. Now, let me get something from you, shit!" she spat, trying to convince her nephew he was his own man.

Dirty went into his pocket and pulled out a sandwich bag filled with pieces of off-white stones. He picked out a slab weighing a gram and gave it to her.

Crystal hadn't expected anything more than a piece worth 20 dollars. She had come off better than expected.

"Here. That's eleven dollars. I thought it was fifteen." She unraveled the crumbled bills, extending the money.

"Yea, I bet you did. Ont need yo' money. That's on the house, but it's the last time. Fuck it! If Ty finds out, he just finds out. But yeen't bout to keep holding shit over my head," Dirty asserted. All he wanted was a clear conscience while his grandmother was lying in the hospital.

Moon opened the screen door to check his yard after hearing some commotion. Crystal had turned her back, making her way through the dark.

"You good, nephew?"

"Yea, I'm good," Dirty replied, watching his aunt cut through a dirt path between the trees.

***

Joanne's nerves were no better than they were before she had smoked the cigarette. She was still standing on the front porch scrutinizing the neighborhood traffic.

Young adolescent males and females could be seen mingling in the middle of the street under the streetlights as usual. They gossiped and joyfully played amongst each other. Nearby, a woman emerged from the dirt trail and walked past the kids enjoying their Friday night.

"Cryssy! That's Crystal's ass coming around the corner. I know that chicken-head-ass walk from a mile away. She must be going to her momma house to smoke that shit. This my chance to go down there and straighten this shit out before Ty get back."

Joanne stepped inside to trade in her house slippers for her pink and blue Nike Air Max 90's. She pulled and wrapped her long ponytail into a bun. Then, she threw on a thin zip-up Nike tracksuit to match.

Joanne left the big screen tv on Lifetime and exited her home. She stepped off the porch on a mission. No need for a car; she walked towards Mrs. Hunter's home, hoping she'd find Crystal there.

With her hood pulled over her head, she made it to the brick house's door. She knocked hard enough to break a meditating monk's peace of mind.

"Who the fuck? Fat ass Tracey must've seen me. I hope she got some good shit and not that mess that be clogging up the stem again." Crystal scurried to the door.

In a rush, she twisted the doorknob without asking who it was on the other side.

"It's me," a familiar voice exclaimed.

Joanne pushed past the door as Crystal backed up, letting her in. She sighed and crossed her arms, ready for her uninvited guest to make a swift exit.

"Dirty ain't here," Crystal spat.

"I'm not here to talk to Dirty. I'm here for you." Joanne pulled the hood off her head.

"We ain't got nothing to talk about," Crystal assured with a disdained look on her face.

Crystal turned her back and walked towards the kitchen. Joanne closed the house door and followed behind her.

"Yes, we do, Cryssy! That shit you saw earlier needs explaining. You see, yo' nephew, Dirty –,"

"Dirty? Ohhh, you want to put it off on him. You the one that's thirty something. You's a grown ass woman. My brother gon' be really fucked up when he finds out it was his nephew's fault that you were sucking his dick in his office!" Crystal assured.

"See, that's the thing. He ain't got to find out. Me and you can work something out between the two of us." Joanne prayed silently after making her plea.

Joanne stuck her hand on the inside of her jacket. Crystal watched her diligently. From the inside of her bra, Joanne pulled out a stack of crispy folded bills.

Licking her right thumb, she began to peel away hundred after hundred.

"This is my fair compensation to settle our little family feud. I love you, Crystal. You're my sister."

Crystal erupted in laughter.

"Sister! Bitch you retarded. I guess you figure because I love to smoke crack, you can just buy me off and see yo' way out of this shit. That sister shit was creative, forgive me for having to laugh, hoe," she said, frustrating her brother's fiancée.

"Take the money, Cryssy," Joanne tried again.

Crystal folded her arms as she leaned back onto the kitchen counter.

"Like I said, fuck yo' money, bitch!" she shouted, adding fuel to the fire.

The money soared through the air as Joanne surprisingly rushed Crystal, catching her with a right jab to the face. Unfazed, Crystal wrapped her hands around the throat of Joanne and began to squeeze.

Crystal knew Joanne wasn't a fighter, so she swore to easily put her in her place with a strangle-hold. But she was doing much more than restraining her as Joanne struggled to breathe.

Out of the corner of her eye, Joanne caught a glimpse of a knife set with steel handles, next to the microwave. She reached with her right as her left hand clutched a handful of Crystal's hair.

Crystal felt a ripping pain from her scalp as a patch of her hair was snatched out.

"Aahh, shit! Bitch! Stank ass hoe! I was gone stop choking yo' ass as soon's you calmed the fuck down!" she spat in a rage, then tightened her grip.

Joanne's fingertips inched their way across the countertop. She felt her way around the biggest steel handle in the knife set. They were a gift from Tyrone to his mother on Christmas the prior year. But Joanne had no recollection of that memory as she struck the 9-inch jagged blade into the now wide-eyed Crystal's neck.

Blood splattered from the jugular vein. It stained the wooden fork and spoon on the wall. It shot onto the refrigerator, and the curtains over the sink. Joanne almost slipped on the bloody floor as she retracted the blade from the entry wound.

The trifling sister-in-law held the knife in her grip, frozen in her stance. She gazed at what looked like a scene straight out of a horror flick. She watched Crystal choke on her own blood for a brief moment, then quickly snapped out of her frozen state.

Joanne rushed to pick up the blood-stained one-hundred-dollar bills.

"Wipe off the knife, Jo Jo. Wipe off the knife," she tried counseling herself through it.

A vague rambling could be heard near the front door, startling Joanne. Out of fear, she tucked the knife on the inside of her zip-up hoodie instead of the original plan to rinse it off and toss it on the floor. She fled out the backdoor of the house, leaving the gurgling sound in the distance.

On the front porch, the rambling was nothing more than a neighbor's hungry pit bull deprived of food and love. Crystal fed him from time to time, causing him to come by regularly.

But Joanne wouldn't have noticed the skinny, brindle breed at the least bit as she moved hastily without looking back. Mrs. Hunter's home was strictly in her rearview and an afterthought while she power-walked with her hood pulled over her head.

Chapter 23

Salute

To anyone who had eyes, Moon's trap was doing numbers, proving business was good. Weed, coke, and crack were on the menu. Everything was a must go. Moon was not only smoking his choice of product, he was also getting his piece of the almighty dollar.

Money had occupied Dirty's mind as Mrs. Hunter's condition had become a subconscious issue. He couldn't let any outside obstacle interfere with the business of the streets. It wasn't an option when stick up kids nor the Feds would have sympathy for his sick grandmother.

"Looks like it's just me and you, nephew. You heard anythang from Sa'von?" Moon sparked a little conversation as he and Dirty took time to count their money.

"Hold on. Wait a minute, unc. 40, 60, 80, 95, 1, 2, 3, 4, 5, a band," Dirty tallied up the cash he'd made in the last few hours.

"Oh, Young Sanity went to Columbia, South Carolina to do a show. They paying my nigga, so, you know. Rap money safer than trap money," Dirty explained as he put the rest of the stash in the cabinet.

"Shit, y'all boys don't know nothing 'bout no music. Shit, nephew, I had a rhythm and blues quartet I led back in my day called the Carolina

Moonlights! We used to come out, boom, hit that lil one two step, kill 'em with the spin move, and grab the mic. I swear I...."

Moon's glory days were broken abruptly by a knock at the door. He peeked through the glass at the top of the house's front door.

"It's Fat Boy and Munchie," he announced to Dirty.

Fat Boy stepped in accompanied by Munchie. He had on his chain that dangled near his belly with an iced out fat baby in a pamper as a charm. Munchie wore no more than a heavy diamond bracelet that stood out even amongst his wide 6' 4" frame.

"Gottdamn, Munchie! You still getting breast fed? I swear you done got bigger since last time I seen't you," Moon joked.

"Yea, nigga. And my momma told me to knock yo' ass out if you still got that same loudmouth from back the days," Munchie said without blinking.

"Them fools stay going at it since way back," Fat Boy grinned, tapping Dirty on the shoulder.

"So, what's up with y'all boys?" Dirty said, smacking Fat Boy's hand then, Munchie's.

"Man, I went by the hospital, lil bruh. Auntie Hunter was talking to me, so that's a good sign. I just wanted to let you know, 'cause momma say yeen been by there. You know she been tending to her," Fat Boy informed.

"Early tomorrow. I'll be there with her favorite, white roses in hand," Dirty promised.

"Well, you know me and Munchie bout to hit up club 30 Plus, but we need some of Cali's best though," Fat Boy said, going into his pockets, retrieving a handful of cash.

Dirty lifted a lid off a cookie jar on the counter and pulled out an ounce of weed. The pungent odor instantly shot throughout the kitchen. Fat Boy gave him a couple of hundred.

"Ain't heard shit from Storm all day. Nigga been Quiet Storm for real. Y'all heard nothing?" Dirty asked.

"Nawl. Ain't heard shit. He probably got him a lil ATL freak up in the Marriott. You know God ain't stop making bad bitches when he made Joanne," Fat Boy said, sharing a laugh with Munchie.

"We up outta here though, cousin. Y'all be safe, ya heard." Fat Boy and Munchie made their exit as a couple of customers approached the door.

***

"The work gotta be in the house cause ain't shit in that shed," Smurf said, crawling back towards his gang through the grass.

"Yea, it might be, 'cause they definitely doing they thang. Look at the white Range that them two big niggas hopping in," Blue Bull analyzed from behind the large barrel in Moon's yard.

"Wait, hold it down fo' a sec. I thank I see how we fin freak this," Clutch said as he watched two customers go through the door.

***

"Let me get some ting for a hundred, Dutty," the Jamaican lady with dreads said in a strong island accent.

"I got thirty," Lil Rich, a 28-year-old addict said.

Lil Rich was served by Moon, then he followed the Jamaican lady through the door. Coming from across the street was Pretty Tony towards the driveway with a dub of good weed and a couple of rocks on his mind.

"Fuck all this waiting shit. We put the ratchet to this nigga head. When they open the door, we ambush they ass." Clutch cocked back his black .45 Taurus.

Bandanna Smurf nodded in approval, gripping his .357.

Pretty Tony walked into the dark driveway, whistling the theme song from Andy Griffith. The wind rattled the bushes in the yard, while the mice played near its roots. He didn't seem in a rush, but he clearly wasn't fully alert as he walked with his head down.

Blue Bull emerged from behind the brick wall on the side of the house. As Pretty Tony's foot hit the bottom brick step, the back of his head felt the pressure of the 9mm barrel on his skull.

"Get the door Moon," Dirty said, hearing a knock.

Moon looked through the glass and saw the customer by himself, looking straight ahead. He opened the door, then the screen door. Tony came crashing to the floor from being pushed in the back by Blue Bull.

"It's a hit!" Moon yelled as he ran and dived for the kitchen floor.

Dirty dived into the living room behind the couch to retrieve his .45 M&P handgun. He looked over the couch, saw faces behind gray and white bandannas and began firing.

Clutch ducked behind the counter, holding the gun to Moon's temple.

"Don't make no sudden moves old man," he advised him.

Bandanna Smurf and Blue Bull fired shots through the couch. A bullet hit the brim of Dirty's hat, knocking it off of his waves.

"Shit!" Dirty ducked his head low and fired off rounds over the leather couch.

Dirty looked towards a bedroom door halfway open behind him. Self-preservation was the closest thing to a plan. He crawled fast as shots ricocheted through and off walls. Once inside, he pushed up a window nervously with the bars missing and jumped out.

"Stop shootin'!" Clutch ordered over the unloading.

"The nigga gotta be dead. Do a check!"

Bandanna Smurf moved slowly through the living room. He saw nothing except for a Miami Heat hat on the green carpet. He looked into the bedroom, saw the window open and figured out the rest.

"He gone," he came back with the news.

Clutch aimed the barrel into Moon's right eye.

"Where's the shit at, ol' school?"

"Shit is in yo' ass hoe!" Moon answered disrespectfully, but rightfully so.

Clutch shot him in his left shoulder. Moon let out a manly cry of agonizing pain.

"This nigga suicidal!" Clutch exclaimed.

"You damn right. Salute me or shoot me, nephew," Moon taunted without a single flinch.

"One more time, old school. You are brave. I give you that. But where's the money and the work?" Clutch gave him another chance to make things right with his gang.

Moon laughed a painful joy, knowing he'd lived a life to the fullest and with little regret. On the inside, he even called Dirty a coward. He knew the devil himself wouldn't use Dirty as a soldier in hell. Moon pushed himself up from the floor on his elbow and looked at Clutch in his eyes.

"Finish yo' breakfast, nephew. Finish yo' breakfast, ha ha."

Clutch sent a scathing bullet straight through his right eye, killing Moon instantly. The old player's head collided with the kitchen floor.

"Search the cabinets!" Clutch ordered as he went into Moon's pockets, retrieving wads of cash.

Bandanna Smurf looked in the two cookie jars. He found 18 ounces of cocaine. He opened the cabinets, following his nose. He found three pounds of exotic weed. Blue Bull opened the microwave and found thirty-four thousand in cash. Clutch looked in the oven and found a whole kilo on the middle rack.

"What you wanna do with O.G.?" Smurf asked Clutch, pointing at the surviving addict.

"Please my nigga. Ain't see nothing!" Pretty Tony pleaded.

Without giving Clutch time to answer, Blue Bull shot him twice in the chest, relieving him of his future witness duties.

VNature Rarebreed

Chapter 24

Conflict

Room 23 at the Super 8 motel on New Bern Ave became refuge away from all of the chaos the city might soon be catching wind of. With money to blow and a new heir of confidence, the crew still needed to lay low and tie up some loose ends before the night's out.

"So, why the fuck this nigga wanted us to clip this nigga Quiet Storm over some personal shit anyway? The game 'posed to be strictly business, never personal," Smurf quizzed.

"Man, you ask too many questions. You got yo' cut, right?" Clutch said as Smurf agreed.

"Okay then. That's all that counts. This nigga shoulda been here by now," Clutch added.

"He still pimpin'? Cause, man I hope he brought two, three hoes in that Cadillac. He keep some bad bitches on the stroll. What's up with that one bad bitch he had down here from Detroit? What's 'er name?" Blue Bull quizzed as he pulled out some rolling papers.

Clutch took notice and tossed a box of Swisher Sweets at him.

"Nigga, yeen know? That's the one crib we been casing. That was his bottom bitch," Smurf answered.

"Oh, yea? So, shit personal then," Blue Bull concluded with his attention on Smurf. He watched him pull what looked like an old woman's wig from his duffle bag.

"This might come in real handy when I catch my next vic," Smurf combed through the synthetic hair with his fingers.

"Nigga, where you get that wig?" Clutch questioned aggressively as the wig appeared to be familiar.

Like a dog that pissed inside the home, Bandanna Smurf wore a guilty expression on his face.

"Nawl, don't tell me you doubled back on granny just then when you left in the Impala. Man, yeen kill 'er did you?" Clutch said furiously.

"Nawl, come on, Clutch. I swear to God," Smurf replied.

Clutch jumped up from the edge of the bed. He swung, catching Bandanna Smurf with a right hook to the jaw. Smurf fell backwards off the other bed he was sitting comfortably on.

Clutch looked in the duffle bag and saw thousands of dollars strewn over two handguns. He knew his homeboy was lying whenever he swore to God ever since they were adolescents.

Bandanna Smurf pushed himself upright on his feet and bull rushed Clutch. They both fell, tussling on the next bed as Blue Bull grabbed some popcorn and took a front row seat for the fight.

Clutch had Smurf in a headlock, punching him in his ribs while he took a few to the gut himself. Blue Bull jumped up after seeing enough. He decided to break the two up.

"Let go, Clutch." He tried to separate Clutch's left arm from around his other friend's neck.

"Y'all niggas gon' get our room ran up in! You crazy? Who the fuck is Granny?"

A knock was heard at the door over all the heavy breathing as the guys caught their breath. Clutch pushed Bandanna Smurf off of him as Blue Bull checked the peephole. He opened the door, and their guest stepped in.

"Damn, my baby! Y'all niggas having a Royal Rumble in this hoe? My money at high risk in this type of environment. I need my cut fo' RPD get they hands on it," Buttafly said, chastising with his signature grape blow pop in hand.

"We'll handle this later, nigga," Clutch grilled Smurf, receiving a mutual look.

Clutch went into a dresser drawer where the customary hotel bible sat inside. Beside it, was a small, brown paper bag, full of money. He handed it over.

Buttafly skimmed through the bills with his thumb. He tucked the paper bag on the inside of his purple Kenneth Cole button up shirt after the quick scan.

"You boys did really good. With all the dust y'all done kicked up, that nigga Ty should be home in no time. Y'all can take it back to The Bull City. Y'all mission is complete," he commanded the team.

"Ont know, Butta. I thank I got me a keeper here in The R." Smurf had love written all over his face as he massaged his jaw.

"Some yella hoe named Red Cherry got this hoe strung open. Fool went and put a tracker on her truck. Nigga can't get the needle out his arm," Blue Bull gave his perspective.

"Red Cherry! Red bone Cherry! Spit Bubble Cherry! Used to sock it to my pocket like a Chinese rocket fo' I went to prison for interstate pimpin' bitches," Buttafly reminisced.

Clutch looked at the scorn and distasteful expression on Bandanna Smurf's face and laughed. Then he turned his attention back towards Buttafly.

"Yea, I thank it's time we break camp. Blue and whites might be out there heavy, hawking down every blue Impala right now. Fucking with this knuckle-head-ass nigga right there," Clutch pointed.

Bandanna Smurf declined to put up a verbal dispute. He was more concerned with how many others knew all about the spit bubbles.

"Sound like a plan to me. I'm too fly to get caught up in y'all dusty ass whirlwind. I'm about to burn the road up, gangstas," Buttafly saluted with two fingers, and popped the grape blow pop back into his mouth.

As he walked, the more than colorful figure pulled out his flip phone. He went through his outgoing calls and pressed the contact he was looking for. Joanne answered the phone on the other end.

"Surprise, surprise! Tell me bitch finally came to her senses!"

"Daddy, my hands won't stop shaking!" Joanne sighed.

"What? Yo' hands won't.... What you talking 'bout?" Buttafly quizzed, confused as he descended the stairs.

"I gotta... We gotta go! Tyrone coming back tomorrow. He don't know what I did yet. We need to go back to Detroit and take Ta Ta home before," Joanne stopped herself, realizing the new Apple devices may not be completely safe.

"Shit, you ain't told me what you did yet, either. Why yo' hands shaking?" Buttafly sat on the gray Cadillac leather adjusting his Cartier glasses.

"Never mind. We just got to leave," she replied wiping her tears along with the snot that was building under her nose.

"We ain't going nowhere without that money, Jo Jo," Buttafly insisted.

"Who said we was leaving the money?" Joanne shot back.

"Oh, so, you got the money, baby?" Buttafly became optimistic.

"No, I ain't got it," she disappointed.

"But nothing is better than him handing it over."

"And if he don't?" Buttafly assumed that he knew what she was getting at.

"We'll just have to use a little persuasion."

"And you saying you got the persuasion? How's that?"

"Daddy, I am the persuasion." Joanne left it at that as she pressed end on her touchscreen.

Buttafly pulled past the End Zone Bar towards highway exit 440 headed for destination Bahama Breeze. It was rare that he relied on a blind hand, but he was willing to let the cards fall where they may. High risks reaped high rewards. And Joanne was nothing more than a pawn in his gamble for a big payday.

VNature Rarebreed

Chapter 25

Roadblock

Just as Dirty promised his cousin, Fat Boy, he did what he said he would do. He stopped by Delonica's Flowers and purchased their most elegant bouquet of white roses on hand. Standing outside of the hospital room, Fat Boy's mother, Rhonda, filled him in on some uplifting news.

"The doctors say that the cancer hasn't gotten to where it can't be treated, Antwan. They say they'll have to use a brief radiation process on her and she'll be able to make a significant recovery. Ain't Jesus good, baby?" Aunt Rhonda hugged her huge, sagging breast up against her nephew's chest.

"Can I go in there, Auntie?" Dirty asked.

"Yes, baby. You know she's expecting you," Rhonda implied.

Mother Hunter wasn't asleep but only resting her eyes. The gospel hymn, I Remember Mama by Shirley Caesar, played on the inside of her mind as she hummed, soothing her pain.

Dirty sat the crystal glass vase on the table next to his grandmother. Since her head was tilted to the side, the roses would be the first thing she saw once she opened her eyelids.

Mrs. Hunter's lashes parted ways slowly, and the scenery gradually became clearer. The radiant ensemble of nature adjacent to her was a sure sign that family was present. She smiled and slowly turned her face upright.

"Antwan, you look so tired, and hungry too," she uttered, noticing the dark red bags underneath his eyes.

Dirty hadn't gotten any sleep. It was 7 a.m. and he'd been up ever since he jumped out of Moon's window.

He knew he couldn't run home and risk being followed, maybe even endangering Crystal. Lil Marc let him in through his bedroom window where he sat upright on the floor through the morning.

"What happened, bruh?" Lil Marc drilled for answers but received no feedback. He knew still, that it could only be one of a few things that caused his friend's awkwardness.

"He gone hate me, ma. They both gone hate me," Dirty said from the chair with his palms covering his face in shame.

"Who is he, son?" Mrs. Hunter inquired.

"God....," he paused, then looked into his hands.

"God and Tyrone both."

"No baby. God blessed you to wake up this morning. So, he can't hate you. And The Lord loves all his churrins," Mrs. Hunter spoke in her weakened voice.

Contrarily, Dirty had never woken up as she assumed he did.

"You have faith in The Lord, don't you?" she asked.

Dirty evaded answering that one directly but gave his own philosophy.

"Tyrone is flesh, unlike God. And flesh ain't as forgiven as some spirit. And Moon, he must had been hated then, cause he ain't...," Dirty held those last words out of respect for his grandmother's condition.

Mother Hunter sensed the pain her grandson was enduring. Unfortunately, Moon hadn't woke up this morning and Dirty had begun to doubt the existence of God. And in some way, Tyrone would be displeased with his nephew's choices that were tied to Moon no longer being alive.

Dirty changed the subject. For good reason, he began to feel as if time was not on his side.

"Ma, Cryssy is a good girl up under all of that. Spite every thang she is going through. She and Auntie Rhonda gonna take care of you. I got to leave and stand on my own two." Dirty grabbed Mrs. Hunter's pecan brown wrinkled hand.

The grandmother understood the young adult needed to grow into the knowledge of the man he desired. She gave her grandson her blessing while they both caressed one another's skin. Dirty turned to see Fat Boy's mother smile in appreciation for him stopping by.

"Aunt Rhonda, take good care of her." Dirty embraced, then stepped past his aunt into the hallway.

Lil Marc stood up from his seat in the waiting area.

"Man, what's next, bruh? Everythang straight?" He showed his concern.

"Yea, I'm good. Let's just keep it moving and not talk about it," Dirty said, not wanting to get emotional.

"What's next is, I might as well lay low. You know I left my phone on the counter at Moon's crib? Once I heard them shots, I knew they were gone – Pretty Tony and Moon," Dirty said, pushing the elevator button to the 1st floor.

"Bruh, I gotta tell you something." Lil Marc tapped Dirty's arm as they descended the hospital's levels.

"The other day at school, some crazy shit happened," Lil Marc began as the doors opened.

Both friends stepped one foot out. The youngster was still getting to the point of what he was saying when Dirty caught a glimpse of a gut-wrenching sight.

"Shit! Back on the elevator!" He urged his friend to backpedal before the doors could close.

Raleigh Police were at the service desk asking for a patient's room number. A black female detective in a suit, pointed towards the elevators, then led the march.

"How you know they want you?" Lil Marc asked his mentor.

"Hustler's intuition. You'll get it one day. Plus, she looks like a homicide detective," Dirty replied nervously.

"She was deep as shit with the police too! Ain't no question they was headed our way. Come on third flo'!" Dirty yelled at the elevator for not moving fast enough.

The elevator bell rang as the light lit up on the number 3 above the automated door. They both stepped off in a hurry.

"Which way, Dirty?" Lil Marc quizzed.

"We take the right. That's the other way to the parking deck. We gone jump in the whip and burn out before they notice," Dirty responded, making way to the end of the hall.

"Bust a left, Lil Marc." They both turned in unison.

"Hey! Hey! You come here!" One officer yelled as they all took a quick pace towards the teenagers.

"Fuck!" Dirty exclaimed as the two turned the opposite direction.

Two blue uniformed cops came off the elevator just a few feet away from Dirty and Lil Marc as they got close to the entrance doors. Of the two, a red-haired male officer tackled Dirty. The other policeman stood in front of Lil Marc with his hand on his taser, daring him to run.

"What the fuck am I being arrested fo' lady?" Dirty spat as his face was planted onto the cold hospital floor.

"We'll let you know everything when you get down to the station," the lady detective in the suit answered.

The woman detective had the face of a runway model. Her nails were three dimensional and she looked to be in the wrong profession.

"Check out Little Bow Wow here fo' anythang. If he's clean let the youngster go," she commanded referring to Lil Marc.

Dirty looked back at his young protégé as he was being escorted off. They both made eye contact.

"Intuition, lil bruh! If they ask, you don't know!" Dirty yelled as he was shoved onto the elevator further down the hall.

Chapter 26

Blinded

Tyrone pulled his Altrue Burlap luggage behind him, rushing through the terminal. He needed to locate an airport cab quickly. Even though Joanne had tried her best to remain undetectable on the phone, Tyrone detected high levels of stress in her tone regardless.

"Hey, baby! Things go good in Atlanta?" Joanne tried masking her anxiety by sounding excited.

She sparked up a cigarette, hoping to relieve much of the weight she was carrying mentally. If she spoke too much, she subconsciously felt suspicious. Too little, and it would have the same effect.

"Yea, baby! I got the properties! Ya heard me? I said, proper teeeez, Anne!"

It was nearly a three second delay in Joanne's reaction.

"Oh, that's great, baby!" She said, blowing out the smoke from her Newport.

"Babe, I thought you was quitting the cigarettes? You been doing good," Tyrone quizzed in a worried tone.

Joannes nerves were a wreck and if Tyrone could see through the phone, he'd see her hair was too.

"Anyway, I'm thankin' about letting Fat Boy uncle handle the shop in Raleigh. He got a degree in business and finance. And my cousin in Atlanta, can run one of the two I got down here, while I run the other one," Tyrone ran down his future plans for his soon to be partner for life.

Joanne was doing more listening and smoking than anything. It was normal for her to inquire about what he was doing or who he was doing it with. But it seemed she was more in tune with the menthol stick she was inhaling.

"Everythang okay, baby? You pulling on that cig kind of heavy, ain't you? You don't thank it's 'bout time to call it quits fo' good?"

"I don't know. It's a struggle, Ty. [Swoooohh]" She exhaled again after a short reply.

"We'll work on it. Where's Ta Ta? Let me holler at 'er," Tyrone said, checking on his teenage daughter's whereabouts.

"Oh, she gone. But she'll be here later on."

Joanne was beginning to sound like a robot. She kept her sentences short and simple. Tyrone was accustomed to more dialogue between the two, especially when he was away. He decided to ask a test question to see how she'd react.

"Baby, I can pay extra and get these late tickets to the comedy show tonight at the PNC. You know Mike Epps on his tour."

Tyrone knew that this would be the moment of truth. He waited for her response.

153

"Okay," she said nonchalantly.

"Okay. Okay? That's all? Just okay. Yea, something definitely off. Knowing Joanne, she would've jumped through the phone to kiss me over this nigga," Tyrone thought to himself.

Tyrone scrolled through his flip phone after hanging up with his fiancée, straight to Dirty's number. Joanne wasn't too informative, but he knew he could count on his nephew.

Dirty's phone went directly to voicemail. Fifteen minutes had gone by, and he still hadn't picked up. Worry began to set in.

"Momma! Shit! God, let her be okay. Damn, a nigga only been gone since Thursday. Maybe, I shouldn't had stayed 'til Saturday but my plug said he needed mo' time."

The Pakistan native with the turban on his head looked into the rearview mirror of his cab. He could tell that his customer was antsy for some reason.

"I would go faster my brother. But in this post nine eleven era people would think I was using my car for a suicide bomb on your highways," he said seriously.

Tyrone held up a hundred-dollar bill and waved it so the driver could see it in the mirror.

"Is that Ben Frank I see, brother?" the driver inquired.

"Yes, my foreign brother. It's Franklin himself. Now, put some mustard on it, Muhammed!" Tyrone referred to the gas pedal.

***

Tyrone stepped into a home that felt empty. The television and the stove light in the kitchen were on, but no Joanne or Tanisha in sight.

"Anne! Ba'y, come 'ere!" he yelled to the backroom.

On a normal return, Joanne would come out of the bedroom in something seductive if she hadn't met her lover at the front door already. Her Ford Explorer was in the driveway. That meant, if she wasn't in the home, she'd walked across the street to check on Tanisha.

Tyrone opened Tanisha's bedroom door and switched on the light. Her stuffed animals were neatly placed in strategic positions that only she knew how. He headed out, cutting off the light.

Everything was neat in his bedroom just the way his woman usually kept things. He removed his gun from his waist and sat it on the red oak dresser. He massaged his facial hairs in the large mirror.

"Man, I got to find out what the fuck is going on. I stopped by Momma's house, Crystal ain't come to the door. Momma must be sleep, but I know damn well, Cryssy ain't," Tyrone spoke amongst himself.

"Let me try Joanne again. She can't be nowhere but across the street, I bet," he said, pressing his fiancée's contact.

The Usher song, Confessions blared through loudly as if Tyrone had it on speakerphone. It was coming in so clear that it sounded like it had surround sound. He turned his direction towards the closet where the vocals seemed the strongest.

Tyrone opened the closet door. Joanne's phone was in the small confinement used for storing shoe boxes and hanging clothes as it had sounded. It was sitting on the lap of Joanne, who was sitting in a chair. Hair

mouth was duct taped. Her arms and legs were bound to the wooden chair. And a black Ruger was wedged into the back of her long, jet-black ponytail. The owner of the hand the gun sat in, was Buttafly.

The infamous grape blow pop wasn't going to miss its superstar role. It spun around on Buttafly's tongue, infuriating Tyrone as rage filled his eyes.

Tyrone tightened his jaw and clinched his teeth. He didn't initially know what this was all about, but he was soon to find out. The elephant in the room was just too enormous to go unnoticed. Here it was, a man who he perceived to be a homosexual, holding his woman hostage in his home.

Tyrone grilled the man who he used to provide deals on the product. Buttafly stood in an all-black linen shirt and slacks. Tyrone could tell that prison had given him a little extra muscle along with a confident new edge.

"Come on, Butta. You a dick chaser. You ain't built fo' what come with this shit," Tyrone was straight forward no chaser. His attempt was to use reverse psychology.

"Sorry my niggah. You've been misled. I'm a pimp. I like bitches. I was raised by bitches. So, at times, mu'fuckas like yo'self tend to thank I'm sweet. But in this case, it turned out sweet for me. I may have sacrificed a little integrity, so what."

"Oh, you's a fag fo' sho'. You might have tried to swell up in the pen so you can fool these women, but nigga fuck all that! What the fuck you doing in this closet?" Tyrone exclaimed with much pun intended.

If Joanne's eyes could talk, they would tell it all. On one hand, she felt safe because Buttafly assured her he'd stick to the plan. On the other, she began worrying about the potential bullet to the brain due to Tyrone's unamusing taunts.

"What the hell is Buttafly doing? Just tell Ty to open the safe so we can get this shit over with. I don't want to see any more blood. Dammit, Crystal! Why the fuck did you have to go and ruin things. And, Dirty. He'll end up putting two and two together about what happened to her. But right now, he's got bigger problems in the county jail since I put the police on his trail. It was too sweet for me to resist claiming he killed Moon. It brought me some precious time. I'll be back in Detroit soon and all of this shit I got myself into will be just another black tragedy. Who cares?" Joanne thought in efforts to relieve her guilty conscious.

Chapter 27
Alarms

Tanisha and Camiya stood on the brick porch in the blue-collar Worthdale neighborhood, having girl talk. Unexpectedly, a red and blue car pulled up, causing Camiya's aunt to come to the screen door of her home.

"Um, excuse me, Miya! Who is this lil boy pulling up in front my house with a cab like he grown? It's 9:30 at night. Hope you don't plan on going nowhere," she interrogated.

"You know that's Lil Marc. Ta Ta's boyfriend," Camiya replied.

"Boyfriend? Girl, bye. Y'all need to quit," the aunt looked him up and down from his Bulls hat to the red and white Jordan 4's.

"Hey! How you doing ma'am?" He greeted.

"Ma'am?" she snapped as if insulted by the gesture.

"I'm twenty-eight. Lil boy trynna act like he got manners and shit. Y'all keep the noise down," she said, stepping inside before taking a doubletake at the Bow Wow look-alike.

"Damn, if Dirty could see that ass, he'd be on it," Lil Marc thought to himself, watching the brown skinned woman depart.

"What's going on, Marc?" Tanisha inquired with the type of concern a mature adult would have.

"They got Dirty, Ta."

"They shot – " Tanisha's mind raced, bringing her emotions to a high.

"Nawl, the police. I went with bruh to the hospital to see his grandmomma. They ran up on us in Wake Med," Lil Marc explained.

"Ain't know, Momma Hunter was even in hospital. What they want with Dirty?"

"Yea, what they want with my baby?" Camiya's heart sunk for the one her young body lusted so much.

"On't know if y'all know this, but old man, Moon got kilt last night," Lil Marc broke the news.

The cab driver blew the horn to show his time was of an essence. Lil Marc gestured with his right hand for him to hold on.

"Oh, my God!" Tanisha covered her mouth with her tiny hands.

Lil Marc's phone began to vibrate on his waist and play My City by 200 featuring Shook, Shakei, and Dirt Raw. It was a number he knew all too well for his age - The Wake County jail.

"It's me, lil bruh. Pick up!" Dirty could be heard over the voice operator.

"Bruh, what's good?" Lil Marc spoke first.

"Shit fucked up. She gone bruh," Dirty said, choking up, but remaining tearless in front of the other men in the holding cell.

"You mean, Grandma?"

"Nawl, nawl. I mean, my auntie Cryssy. They killed her too. Police thank I killed Moon. These crackas is crazy!" Dirty banged his knuckles on the glass in the holding cell.

His hand was now bleeding. Seeing this, the other men could tell he was on edge. They gave him his much-needed elbow room so he could vent without any complications.

"Nah, bruh," Lil Marc pinched his forehead.

"What the hell is going on?" he asked as Tanisha and Camiya stood by waiting to be filled in.

"What my cousin saying, Lil Marc? Let me see the phone," Tanisha snatched it from his hands.

"Hello! Hello? Damn, I thank he hung up."

"Nawl, you hung up when you grabbed the phone," Lil Marc retorted.

"Damn, Ta Ta, moving so damn fast and shit! I miss him!" Camiya folded her arms and pouted.

"The police saying he kilt Moon. And even worse, ont thank I even wanna tell you. Y'all already heard enough," Lil Marc elaborated halfway.

Tanisha grabbed a handful of his short sleave Polo. She tugged and stretched it, trying to shake the information out of him.

"What the fuck he said, nigga, shit!" she insisted.

"Cryssy was found dead at home. Somebody killed her too," Lil Marc said, then grabbed Tanisha and hugged her tight.

"Oh, my God!" Camiya said, now holding her hand over her mouth as well.

"Nobody know what the hell is going on, Ta Ta. But we need to go check on yo' mom," Lil Marc advised.

"Oh, shit! I'm trippin'! Let me call her now," Tanisha pulled out her phone.

Joanne's phone rang continuously without a response. Tanisha looked at her friends with a vague expression as the voicemail played. In that same moment, she had a premonition.

"Come on, let's go!" she brushed past Lil Marc towards the red and blue cab.

"Hold on, Ta. I gotta get my stuff," Camiya said from the steps.

"No. You stay here just in case we need you. I'm going to the house!" Tanisha yelled, then rushed into the backseat.

"What's up, Ta Ta? What's on yo' mind?" Lil Marc said as he sat beside her.

"You probably guessing the same shit," he added.

Tanisha looked back at her teenage love as they both locked eyes.

"BUTTAFLY!" they both said in unison.

***

Buttafly looked at his black and gold Movado watch. It stated that it was time to cut the small talk short. 9:45 was the specific time and measure to bring things to a close.

"Take a wild guess. Why else would I be fresh out the state penitentiary, standing in front of a hidden safe, with a gun to yo' bitch? It's simple

161

mathematics, baby," Buttafly slurped the grape flavored juice from his lollipop.

***

"Call Fat Boy, Lil Marc. Tell him and Munchie meet us at the house," Tanisha commanded.

"Ta Ta, you know ain't got Fat Boy number. Them niggas look at me like a kid. Yo' pops stayed kicking me out Moon's trap, telling me to go home and shit!"

"You right. Well, call Sa'von! Call somebody, damn!" Tanisha gave Lil Marc a punch to the shoulder out of desperation.

"Damn, Ta! He gone out of town on some rap music shit. Looks like it's just me and you. Don't worry though. I'ma hold us both down just the way Dirty raised me!" Lil Marc grabbed Tanisha's hands to calm her nerves.

Chapter 28

Burned

"That's that fat nigga from the spot we ran up in where the old man was at!" Smurf conversed with himself as he ducked low in the BMW.

Fat Boy stepped down from the driver's side of the white Range Rover and walked towards Red Cherry's SUV. He pulled her door open, and she greeted him with a peck on the cheek as she stepped out.

Bandanna Smurf's eyes grew wide and suspenseful as the ashes dropped onto the lap of his jeans.

"Cherry, what the fuck you doing, bitch? I just gave you that money this afternoon. Now, she trynna handle me like a lame!"

The peck on the cheek turned into sloppy wet tongue action, then on to frisking Fat Boy's manhood. The percentage of the two making it to the room in the Marriott hotel seemed next to slim as Bandanna Smurf looked on.

"Damn, baby! You thank we gonna make it up the elevator?" Fat Boy had to pry his tongue from her mouth.

Red Cherry palmed his shimmering charm with a fat baby in a pamper. She tested the heaviness in her hand as if her palm was a weight scale.

"I'm sorry, baby. You was just looking so tasty. I had to have a lil bit right then and there. We can move it along now," Cherry said, twisting seductively in front as she led the way.

A Priscilla's adult novelty bag dangled from Red Cherry's hands. Bandanna Smurf nearly blew his cover as he turned his body to follow their trails, watching through the back window.

"Priscilla's! Oh, hell nawl, bitch! How my dick and ass taste mu'fucka?" Smurf ranted.

Bandanna Smurf needed to stay as far away from gasoline as possible. He was on fire, seeing Red Cherry just finish groping another man's package. He watched the two enter into the lobby as he shut the car door without slamming it.

He began to follow at a safe distance as if he was undercover. Fat Boy and Red Cherry walked past the female clerk, and he assumed that they had their room already. They continued to fondle each other teasingly until the elevator doors opened. Bandanna Smurf slid past the two unnoticed as Cherry's back was turned.

"On the elevator? Yeen't got time, baby," Fat Boy declined.

Red Cherry unzipped his pants quicker than the doors could close. She got down on her knees. Fat Boy was feeling woozy from the ride ascending, but equally excited from the unbelievable head he was receiving.

Bandanna Smurf rode furiously, passing the seventh floor as he watched from the other see-through elevator to come to a stop. Having to endure his sights was just too much to stand.

They were both too tied up in their public display of affection to notice they were being spied on. Fat Boy cuffed the back of Red Cherry's hair, thrusting himself deeper into her throat. He fell limply up against the wall. The elevator slowed before coming to a halt.

"The elevator, oh, oh, shit! Hold on, baby!" Fat Boy tapped on her shoulder, barely able to speak.

Red Cherry was incoherent as she handled her business. She did a grinding pepper motion with her hands as she swallowed him whole like a pro.

Fat Boy was tugging at his pants. Red Cherry was licking the precum from the head of his swollen tip. The doors opened up once the 12 up above illuminated.

"Look at this nigga running fast as fuck on the other side. Look like he coming this way," Fat Boy said as they walked toward their room.

Red Cherry tilted her head low to hide when the face became more obvious.

"Bitch! Let me get my money!" Smurf yelled, as he noticed the dust on her knees.

Fat Boy took his gun off of his waist. Instincts told him things would get confrontational.

"What the fuck you doing, niggah? Are you stalking me?" Red Cherry shouted, standing tall in her heels.

"Yea, bitch! Now, up my money!" Smurf said, holding his right palm out.

"Let us by, homie," Fat Boy said, grabbing Red Cherry by the waist.

"Let you by? Nigga, what?" Smurf reached for the gun he had in his waistband.

Fat Boy lunged for his Smurf's wrist to keep him from aiming the gun. He hit him with a heavy blow to the side of his jaw with his right fist. A shot rippled towards the elevator that was still open, and they both fell onto the hallway floor.

Red Cherry screamed as she ran for the elevator doors. It closed her inside and she pushed the ground level button.

Fat Boy's weight was too much for Bandanna Smurf. He'd have to get the advantage over the gun and shoot him to get from underneath him. The two were battling for dear life and neither had much of a clue why.

Fat Boy was overpowering Bandanna Smurf. While holding the arm with the gun at bay, Fat Boy reached for his own with his free hand. A loud pop sounded throughout the 12th floor and blood commenced to soak the carpet.

Bandanna Smurf stopped fighting as Fat Boy hurried to his feet and looked himself over for blood.

Red Cherry saw Fat Boy step off the elevator in an urgent pace as he moved towards the lobby. She hung up her phone.

"Who the hell was you calling?" He grabbed her by the elbow.

"I don't know. The police."

"Is you crazy? Come on! I knew you was trouble," Fat Boy said, pulling her towards the exit doors.

A young female desk clerk watched from the counter the couple make their retreat. In between sexting her boyfriend nude pics and dirty thoughts, she wasn't aware of the 12th floor drama.

A bloody palm smacked the clerk's counter, frightening her. It lost its grip and left a trail of blood as the body collapsed to the floor. The young lady threw down her phone and ran to his side.

Bandanna Smurf was still breathing. She rushed back behind the desk and called 911, requesting an ambulance.

He had willed the strength to make it onto the elevator after getting shot in his side. As he lay near the counter, fighting for his life, he vowed to never again chase the Red Cherry's of the world.

Chapter 29

Eye's Wide

Lil Marc and Tanisha pulled up to the curb in the cab. Their little hearts were racing, but both felt up to the task.

"You two be safe," the African cab driver said as he received forty dollars for his patient service.

Thinking he would leave the kids with a positive word went ignored. Neither teenager responded as they both rushed from the backseat. Lil Marc slammed the car door as he was the last out.

"He back!" Lil Marc noticed the black Cadillac CTS-V shining under the moonlight.

"Yo' momma is okay, Ta Ta," the youngster showed his optimism as Tanisha scrambled through her purse for her house-key.

"God, she better be," the worried girl hoped as she rattled the key into the lock.

It was only wishful thinking. Tanisha knew that one of the first things her stepfather did was inquire of her whereabouts when he came home. Seeing his car in the driveaway, but never receiving that phone call, didn't sit well with her. It sent chills up her spine.

Lil Marc cocked back his small pistol and held it in his pocket. Tanisha looked back at him inquisitively.

"You know, just in case," Lil Marc confirmed.

***

"Okay. You got it, Butta. You the man right now," Tyrone threw up his hands in surrender.

"I'm only doing this for the woman's sake. Step aside." He brushed past Buttafly's shoulder in the small space.

Tyrone kneeled down and grabbed the safe's rotating dial. Buttafly positioned himself in front of Joanne, facing the back of the man who once had control of his home. He was even nice enough to turn her around to witness the event's grand finale.

Tanisha and Lil Marc crossed into the confines of the home. It was cool and quiet, but unsettling and eerie.

Tanisha made a motion to yell her mother's name. Lil Marc muffled her call with his left hand just in time. Only a small screech made it through.

"Shhhhh! Use yo' head, Ta. I thank somebody's in the crib," he uttered lowly as he pulled out his gun.

They both tip-toed towards the couple's bedroom. The door was halfway open. Tanisha had never known for them to have sex with the door open. She silently agreed with her young friend that someone other than usual was inside.

Tyrone turned the dial to the last number. The chambers loosened and the door inched open.

"Open up! Open up the safe all the way!" Buttafly yelled.

Tanisha cringed as she heard the sound of the all too familiar voice in her home.

"It's him!" she held onto Lil Marc's arm in fear.

"I told you not to worry," he kissed her on the cheek.

The two youngsters moved silently into the threshold of the lion's den. They could see Buttafly's back turned towards them as he stood in the closet. Someone was being held at gunpoint in a chair.

Tanisha wanted to scream once she saw her mother tied up, but she felt helpless. Lil Marc signaled for her to back out if it was too much to handle. She refused and gathered her nerves together.

Tyrone opened the black door made of steel all the way. Buttafly's eyes grew wide as his endorphins rose.

A little black velvet box sat at the edge of the safe. There was no money on the inside. Not a dollar. Not a dime. Nor a brand-new copper penny with the man who allegedly freed the slaves.

Buttafly became enraged.

"What the fuck is that?" he yelled.

Tyrone grabbed the box, turned himself towards Joanne. If he was going to die, he wanted to confess his love to her if it was the last thing he did.

He opened the box and stood up. Going out on his knees wouldn't be Tyrone "Quiet Storm" Hunter's legacy. The platinum ring with a 3-carat diamond was flawless. Hunter was engraved on the inside of the band. Joanne couldn't help herself from blushing even with the tape strapped to her mouth.

"He does really want to marry me! I let my insecurities get the best of me. That little girl that once turned favors for money was like the devil on my shoulder. It was jealous of the new me. But I see, I should have known I have everything I need in Tyrone Hunter."

A single tear escaped from Joanne's right eye.

Buttafly unwedged the gun from the back of Joanne's ponytail. He aimed it at Tyrone.

"A rang mane? A fucking rang, nigga! Ain't nobody getting married after this shit!" Buttafly swore as his index finger applied pressure on the trigger.

PAP! PAP! PAP!

The slender bullets pierced through Buttafly's back barely missing his spinal cord. He turned around to see who would have the audacity.

"Lil Bow Wow," he pointed the grape lollipop.

Buttafly laughed demonically as a trickle of blood drained from his mouth.

Lil Marc was about to shoot again, until the gun fell from Buttafly's hand. He dropped to the floor, clutching his stomach as blood left his body slowly.

"Lil Marc, Ta Ta! What tha?" Tyrone wiped the sweat from his brow.

The young buck he used to kick out of the trap house had just unexpectedly saved the life of his and Joanne's. Now, he was forever grateful.

"I gotta give you a salary, lil homie. Might even owe you back pay," Tyrone said seriously.

Chapter 30

Last Dance

After the wedding, Tyrone sent Tanisha and Lil Marc back on a flight with Fat Boy and the rest of the family. This was their time to reflect as the sun began to set. He and Joanne wanted to walk the beautiful sandy beaches of Bimini to enhance their romantic evening.

Tyrone held Joanne's soft brown hands with masculine hands of his own. He held the celebration bottle in the other.

"Baby, your legs tired of walking yet?" Tyrone inquired with such compassion for his newly married spouse.

"No, baby. Just a few more minutes in the sand. It feels so good in between my toes. Baby, do you thank that they'll be able to clean my dress after this? Look. It's got water and sand all over –"

Tyrone kissed her lips before she could finish her sentence. Joanne's heart melted and her lower lips became beyond moist. Their tongues intertwined like never before and she almost collapsed into his strong embrace.

"Anything you ask for, I'll do. That's what I meant when I said for better or worse, and I'm not going back on my word," Tyrone said, staring his piercing dark eyes into her chinky ones.

"So, anythang else you need, 'cause I'm right, here, baby," he warmly smiled.

"Baby, I'm fine. Everythang is more than perfect. I thank I'll sit down now and rest my feet," Joanne took Tyrone up on his initial offer.

"Listen to you. Every thang. And thank? Girl, you don' got country, my baby," Tyrone laughed as he took her hand.

Joanne took a seat as Tyrone aided her on the shore. Joanne winced as she was trying to get comfortable.

"Ouch!" she yelped lightly.

"What, baby? I couldn't hear you over this beautiful sounding wind. What is it? A cramp? Something on the ground?" Tyrone quizzed, looking around for a creature nearby in the sand.

"Uh, no. I said, oh! As in, oh, I forgot to do something very important," Joanne smiled convincingly.

"And what could that be? You acting real busy-body right now. We made it! It's a celebration, baby," Tyrone said, turning up the bottle of Dom Perignon Champagne.

"I got to make a wish," Joanne replied.

"Well, close yo' eyes and make a wish, baby. It's that simple" Tyrone suggested.

"Not like that, baby. I'm serious. I want to walk into the ocean in my wedding dress. Hey, you said I could get it cleaned," Joanne massaged her husband's smooth brown face.

"It's yo' day, baby. Better yet, it's yo' world!" Tyrone leaned in to help his wife up, then kissed her on the lips.

He released Joanne's hand, and she began to walk towards the water barefoot. Tyrone watched, mesmerized by the way everything was beginning to feel like a happy ending to a movie. The sky was full of radiant colors, purple, orange, pink, and blue. And he couldn't believe that unlike his father and countless others, he had survived and beat the system.

The ghostly visions of Jip no longer plagued his conscious, but two very special people did.

"Moon, I wish you could have been here O.G., you ol' freak. It was sho' nuff some fine women that came to see yo' nephew just hot-jump the broom. I did have the decency to save you some champagne though," Tyrone took a sip from the bottle of champagne, then poured some out into the sand for his friend.

"And sis', I miss you Cryssy. They gon' rot in hell for what they did to you. I know now that Buttafly had something to do with you and Moon leaving us too soon. Damn, that nigga wanted to live my life that bad. I'm sorry I wasn't there for either of you," Tyrone sulked, thinking of the void he now had.

Joanne's feet crossed from land into water. The light wind pushed the waves between her thighs, giving her a wonderful sensation. She looked back at Tyrone in the distance. He looked so peaceful and serene. She stuck her right hand up under her dress and retrieved what had brought her discomfort.

"Ah, there you go, baby! I flew you out all the way from North Carolina to the Bahamas so we could finally part ways," Joanne smiled deviously, holding the knife with an eight-inch blade.

"Well, I said that I was going to make a wish, didn't I? I wish that you wash far far away until you wash up on the shores of Africa some-damn-where. But I never want to see you in this lifetime again."

Joanne dipped the knife into the water and let it go as the tide pulled it in. With the murder weapon clear out of the picture, it would be nothing for her to start over with a clean slate. Although, Dirty would have his assumptions about what may have transpired that night, she'd simply tell her husband this;

"Baby, me, a killer? That's ridiculous!" Joanne practiced before signaling to Tyrone that she was on her way.

Chapter 31

The Letter

Eleven months into his bid, Dirty was finally making transitions in life that were contrary to his past. The reading bug, math bug, and black history bug bit him all at the same time. By his words, his young protégé could see some of the changes for the better.

Lil Marc,

What it be like, lil bruh? I know you ain't heard from your brother in a minute. Shit, it's been damn near a year now. I got your letter this Thursday though.

I got them pics you sent me hanging up on the wall. You and my lil cousin, Ta Ta look good together in the one with y'all at the beach. What's it like in the Bahamas? That was a perfect spot for my uncle to get married at. Him and Joanne look happy together. I'm glad cause I swear ain't thank it was gonna happen.

You know ain't got but bout six months left on this state conspiracy charge. Salty ass Detective Hassleblack had two indictments on a niggah. They couldn't checkmate the king, so they settled for a knight. Then they brought up some old janky ass assault charges against me. Fuck it though, it's better than getting charged for a murder that ain't do.

But check it, lil bruh. A niggah got his GED up in here. I finally made my momma proud. Them doctors that treated her cancer gave hope and inspiration to a young jitterbug. Momma living with Fat Boy's mom now so, she's taken care of.

Y'all showing out in them pictures of you and Young Sanity down in Atlanta. I see y'all boys looking icey too, bwoi! Who them broads all on cutty nuts though now that he got a deal and shit. I'll fuck the shit out that one hoe with that green skirt on. I wonder how much they gave that niggah. Fool prolly swear he pretty now. Oh, I hope y'all niggahs ain't out there rocking them skinny jeans either or I'm gon clown y'all loc ass.

Another thang, lil bruh. You know my unk ain't got nothing but good thangs to say about you these days. You came a long ways from getting kicked out of Moon's trap. Damn, rest in peace O.G.

When I see you, we gon kick it like we used to. But right now, I gotta keep my priorities in perspective. Yeah, check out the vocabulary my niggah. Them streets is asinine. Stay out of trouble, lil bruh. We in some good company right now with the fam breaking into all these new ways to get money legally.

Damn, I almost forgot, bruh. Tell Camiya I done got swole up in here. A niggah got muscles everywhere. But I got to give her bout three more years now since she only just turnt fifteen and shit.

Love lil bruh,

Dirty

"Aaaah, ha, ha! Damn, my nigga a fool still! I can't wait 'til he come home!" Lil Marc said, remembering the good times and thinking of the future good days to come.

He folded up the letter and put it in his jeans pocket. Tanisha was shaking her head at the last couple of lines Lil Marc read out loud. Her friend, Camiya's face was proof that everyone didn't think Dirty was funny.

"Come on Miya. You know he was just playing, girl. Why you gotta be so sensitive?" Tanisha stopped giggling to comfort her best friend.

"Nawl. But how is he gonna say all that about my age after his ass already broke the law? And on top of that, that sorry ass nigga never got them Jordans either," Camiya felt ashamed.

"Don't worry, Miya. You know Antwan. He talking that I changed prison mess, but deep down inside, he ain't nothing but the same ol' Dirty," Tanisha replied, then hugged Camiya.

VNature Rarebreed

About The Author

Once an inspiring rap artist Lil V Nature, my album is called It's N My Nature available on various platforms. Go download that asap! I'm also the author of a mystery-suspense-thriller, Bartholomew, which is doing great numbers and getting great reviews. Go purchase that the fast way. I'm from Raleigh, NC born and raised. I'm late to the creative game due to a 12-year 7 month fed bid. I'm playing catch up right now. But I'm doing it the right way. I'm hoping to inspire those who are where I've been to write and express themselves. And hopefully, deter those who are headed down the wrong path to find their true talents. Everybody has one or many. Nobody is born with none. Stay tuned for interviews, merchandise, content, and anything I have next under the VNature Rarebreed brand.

Nature

VNature Rarebreed

1130 Garner Rd. 27601 Raleigh, NC

michaelboss-es.inteletravel.com

Instagram: @ghslwear

Made in the USA
Columbia, SC
06 April 2025

56134154R00107